E.W. Farnsworth

Engaging Rachel

Engaging Rachel

E.W. Farnsworth

For permission requests, write to the publisher at the address below:
Attention: Permissions Coordinator
Zimbell House Publishing, LLC
PO Box 1172
Union Lake, Michigan 48387
mailto: info@zimbellhousepublishing.com

© 2015 E.W. Farnsworth
Cover Design by The Book Planners
www.TheBookPlanners.com

Published in the United States by Zimbell House Publishing, LLC
http://www.ZimbellHousePublishing.com
All Rights Reserved

Print ISBN: 978-1-942818-41-0
Kindle ISBN: 978-1-942818-42-7
Digital ISBN: 978-1-942818-51-9
Tradepaper ISBN: 978-1-945967-30-6
Library of Congress Control Number: 2015954286

First Edition: November/2015

10 9 8 7 6 5 4

Dedication

For Nadine

Contents

Rachel the Raw Recruit

Call me Anderson. It is not my real name. People in my business do not have real names. Real names always lead to trouble. One of Shakespeare's better characters asked, 'What's in a name?' and nothing good came from that. Anyway, my story is not about names or my many names. It is about the most remarkable woman I ever met. I never knew her real name. I gave her the name Rachel as an inspiration. A friend later told me that the name Rachel had been used in the Old Testament of the Bible, but that is not where I got the name for her. My Rachel was five-nine. She had long, black curly hair, flashing black eyes, a knockout figure and a face right out of the high fashion magazines. I cannot imagine the biblical Rachel as having anything but her raven-black hair.

I was driving through downtown Los Angeles when I rammed the brakes. On the street corner was a female vision holding a white sign with bold black letters that read "Ride?" Well, now. Let's see what we have here. I gestured for her to climb into my Jaguar. She smiled as if she were ascending into heaven. She danced in front of my car to reach the passenger side and climbed aboard. When seated, she gave me a direct, appraising look. She was dressed in ragged blue jeans, a white T-shirt, and old-fashioned high-top Keds. For flair, she wore a red bandana tied around her neck. She wore no makeup, and her hair was made into two braids. In her lap was a denim sack tied at the top with a drawstring.

"Mister, thanks for picking me up. You have a nice Jag."

I nodded appreciatively while I admired her.

"Right up front, I have no home and no family and no diseases that I am aware of. I have been standing on that stinking corner all morning long, and I hate being on my feet. I'm dead tired, dead broke and downright famished. Now that you know all about me, where do we eat?"

I felt a bit frazzled by the information overload. The honking horns behind us were like an infernal fanfare, so I pulled off slowly and considered the options and the odds.

"All righty then, we'll begin at the nearest hamburger joint and go from there."

The woman was bouncing up and down like a little girl all the way into the restaurant. I told her to order whatever she wanted. When she did that, she excused herself to go to the john to pee. She found me with our food at a table in a dark corner away from the windows. Her seat put her beautiful face in full view. From the ravenous way she dived into her meal, I thought that she might not have eaten for at least two days. I remained silent while she ate to give her time to get used to my presence. She did not seem to mind my eyes watching her natural grace and total lack of inhibitions.

She did not focus on me at all until she had finished her triple cheeseburger and fries and was working the straw in the last half of her giant Coke.

"Do you always pick up girls on the street?"

"I always pick up women like you, but you're the first one ever." She genuinely laughed.

"So, well, why did you pick me up? To get me into bed? You're pretty good looking, and you look straight, I guess I owe you that much for this meal." She was smirking, half seductively.

"I've something much more complex and interesting in mind than leaping into the sack with you."

"I definitely don't like the sound of that, mister. What do you mean?"

"Look, I'm not a pimp or a criminal. I'm a talent spotter, but not for the movies. I don't know precisely how to say this, but you've got talent that would not look right on a typical resume. I want to walk through an idea with you to see what you think about it."

She considered this for a moment and bit her lip.

Then she asked, "Can we talk about it at a motel where I can shower and sit in a chair with a cushion?"

So we split from the hamburger dive and went back through the tyrannous Southern California sunshine to the first seedy motel we spied. We checked in there as Mr. and Mrs. Smith. Our room was painted a dingy brown and looked like it had been decorated by Bram Stoker. It did have a shower that worked, and that was enough for my female companion, who ran the hot water, stripped all her clothes off without a moment's delay right in the main room in front of me, to my utter astonishment and delight, and stepped naked into the clouds and rain of the enclosure. The enclosure door snapped shut, but I could follow her motions through the glass like an abstract art color video.

Ace intelligence operator that I was, I noticed that my initial impression was correct. She was most certainly a woman. She had all the right equipment in all the right places. The way she moved and walked, she was a natural with no consciousness of her effects. I, on the other hand, was very much conscious of her effect on me. I was visibly aroused and thinking of ways to maneuver this living, breathing goddess into the waiting, freshly made bed. *But wait a minute. My aim is recruitment, not self-indulgence.* I told the woman that I had not intended to bed her, but that was in the street, and this was different, wasn't it?

From the enclosure, the woman asked, "Care to join me in the shower?"

I didn't ask her whether that was a trick question. Instead, I gallantly said, "I'll wait outside for you to finish and dry yourself."

In a cheery voice, she said, "Your choice! Last chance!"

I watched her step out of the shower and dry herself unselfconsciously in a timeless process that might have been captured by Renoir or Degas, or by Lysippus the Greek. The vision of her toweling herself after her shower alone was worth the cost of the meal and the motel. When she had finished, she wrapped one large terrycloth towel around herself and secured another around her still-damp hair. She ran water in a glass and came to sit in the comfortable chair by the window with her glass of water. Sitting in the chair with her legs buckled back underneath her behind, she made direct eye contact now with a look of confidence and pride. While she shook her head and cocked it to look at me appraisingly, the woman seemed self-assured and took out one of my cigarettes and let me light it for her.

"Thanks for the meal and the shower. I feel almost human again. So tell me, what's your idea?"

"I'll lay out the idea, and while you're thinking about it, you can take a nap. Meanwhile, I'll go out and buy you some new clothes. The clothes you just took off are the worse for wear."

She smiled a crooked smile and nodded. So I began with my usual line.

"Some work is necessary but cannot be advertised. The work I have in mind for you requires special people who don't like leading the normal lives of normal people.

"Well, that describes almost everyone, doesn't it?" She seemed amused and twisted her hair between her fingers. She was not dumb, my Rachel. I patted myself on the back for choosing a tigress.

"My work is very secret." Rachel nodded, expecting that. So I went straight to the point.

"You have all the physical qualities that would be needed for a special job I have for you to do. If you do well, we'll discuss your doing further work with me. If you want out, you can just walk. The only proviso is that you can never tell anyone what you have done or that you were connected to me when you did it. Do you have any questions?"

"Tell me straight up, will I have to kill anyone?" She said this hesitantly.

"That would depend on the circumstances, but the choice would be yours, not mine."

"What do you intend to pay me?" This was a good sign that she was seriously considering what I was telling her.

"I'll pay you fifteen thousand dollars in cash in unmarked bills for three nights' work, whether you spend all three nights doing it or not."

"Hmm. Will the job require rough sex, blue or brown sex, or violence? Group sex or sex with women?" Her questions were asked in a matter-of-fact manner. She knew the lingo and apparently wanted the rules of engagement spelled out. She wasn't smiling now, and her eyes locked onto mine. She leaned forward for my answer.

"You won't necessarily encounter any of these things. You'll have to ingratiate yourself with the target and to perform sex with him as if you were deeply and passionately in love. I do want to warn you that you will be in some danger, but I'll back you up and take care of any problems that arise. So are you interested in the job?" I thought she relaxed a little at my concern for her safety. She recrossed her legs and sat back a little. Her eyes softened, and she drummed her fingers animatedly. I was now cautiously optimistic that we were close to a deal.

"I'll naturally need to know more, but I'm willing to listen further."

I spent some time describing the work she was to do, including my expectations that she would always use her initiative to gather information about her target by any means. She understood what I said about gathering intelligence, periodic reporting and working so that she would not be suspected as a spy. Essentially, I briefed her on Intelligence 101 with a particular focus on her immediate assignment. She appeared to be following everything I told her. When I was sure she knew what she needed to know for tonight, it was time to arrange for her costume.

"Look, I need to buy your clothes now, so I need your measurements. Fair enough?"

"That's the first ridiculous thing you've said. No man could ever buy what I need. I'll take a few minutes to shave my legs and dress in my old clothes. Then I'll go with you to shop for my new wardrobe. Fair enough?"

"I'll absorb the cost, and the amount I spend on your clothes will be in addition to your pay. We'll also go to a salon to have your hair shampooed and done up and for you to have a mani-pedi. We'll have you made up in a natural fashion because that will please your target. Before we start out, by what name should I call you?"

She hesitated and bit her lower lip.

"I'll call you Rachel. Okay?"

She smiled, thought about the name for a minute and nodded—and that was that.

Our day downtown yielded a complete makeover for Rachel: evening wear with stockings, heels, jewelry, a comfortable daytime outfit with flats, and jeans with a T-shirt and kerchief that matched what she wore when I picked her up. After her makeover, Rachel appeared completely natural—and ravishingly beautiful. Rachel was a knockout in her new blue chiffon evening dress with the topaz necklace. When she paraded her dress for me at the store, she might have stepped right off a high-fashion runway. Before we left the store, Rachel had changed into the new jeans, T-shirt and Adidas running shoes that I had bought for her. She wanted to purchase a handbag and toiletries, and I gave her the money to do that. My expenses for the day were under three thousand dollars. We threw her old clothes into a handy donation bin.

When we returned to our motel, we were ready to plan Rachel's mission in earnest. I ordered in the Chinese language for us both and said we would eat with chopsticks. While we ate, I explained what I wanted her to do for me.

"The action will begin at nine p.m. tonight at an expensive martini bar off the strip. This motel room will be our fallback rendezvous. It is also the place where you'll be paid."

She nodded as she ate a broccoli floret with beef gravy.

"I expect you to make contact with your target in the bar. You'll go to his home tonight and stay there for the next two days and nights. All you have to do after you make contact is keep the target engaged and watch for anything that he has to do with a Mexican named Delgado. I'll be watching the entire action, but you won't see me."

I stopped at this point. I held up a cell phone and passed it to her. "Here is a special cell phone. My cell number is set as speed dial number one. When you call me, press the pound sign just before you speak the first time. That makes our calls secure."

She considered this for a moment, then asked, "Do I press pound when you answer?" I nodded affirmatively. "And I don't need to press pound at the end of the call?" I shook my head indicating that she did not.

"Unless you have any questions, let's finish our dinner and then get ready to go."

David Hartnet, a clean-shaven, dark and handsome man, was sitting at the bar alone drinking tequila with ice and looking glum—as if he had just lost his only friend. I walked into the bar with Rachel and turned her towards David. It was that simple. Rachel homed in on her target. She closed right inside his personal zone, batting her eyes at him mournfully as if she were in distress and looking for his attention. In seconds, Hartnet recognized her presence and looked up in amazement. She told him something and looked down at the bar and waited. He waved at the bartender to bring her a drink and him a refill. He was suddenly smiling at her and tucking his fingers under her chin and raising her eyes so he could see them while he spoke. He had taken charge, and she moved even closer to him, brushing her leg against his and making him straighten his back.

To observe them, I kept well back as if I were waiting for someone else to arrive. I tried not to make my surveillance of them obvious, but they were entirely engaged with each other now and oblivious to their surroundings.

David and Rachel spent an hour talking quietly with each other, and then they left on an odyssey that included four other bars and a late night restaurant before they returned to David's house on the beach. There the lights remained on for a while, and then they retired for the night. The next day David left early, and Rachel remained at his house.

Rachel phoned me at noon on the cell phone I had given her and established secure communications by pushing the pound sign as I had instructed.

"The man named Delgado left a message on David's house telephone answering machine. I heard the message saying that the meeting was tonight at 11 p.m. at the warehouse in San Pedro. Delgado said to come alone." She delivered this priceless intelligence in an even tone. I was ecstatic about this critical break in our case. I eagerly awaited more.

"Delgado said he would call David on his cell phone to give further details and see him later tonight. Got all that?" She sounded like she knew the value of what she was imparting. Her tone was businesslike, like a professional spy reporting to her agent runner.

"Yes. Excellent. Anything else?"

"Yes. I searched David's house and found a laptop with a file containing names and many numbers that look like shipping numbers. His laptop has no security that I could detect, so I used one of David's thumb drives to download a copy of this file. I also found a collection of picture files of good looking women. Should I download those to the thumb drive also?"

"Yes, do that if enough memory remains on the stick."

"If that thumb drive doesn't have enough memory left, I'll use another."

"Thanks, Rachel, for taking the initiative. Be sure to clean everything and wipe your prints from his computer so that David won't sense your intrusion."

I might have pulled Rachel immediately because her part was now done, but on a hunch, I hesitated. I did not know what else Rachel could learn, but I wanted her in place as an ace in the hole if Hartnet managed to escape during our raid on the San Pedro warehouse.

My team and I knew precisely where the warehouse in question was located, and I had long wanted information on a shipment destined for it. Now from Rachel, we had the time window we needed. Hartnet and Delgado would both be on scene. I figured that we could take them both down. That was huge. I, therefore, dialed a unique number on my cell phone to alert my operational team.

"Sammy, we take Hartnet, Delgado, and all their people down tonight at the warehouse. Yes, they will all be there. I'll be on scene to lead the raid."

"Anderson, Kerry won't be back in time to join us. Phil will take his place. Okay?"

"No problem. By the way, I'm also arranging for a helicopter with a searchlight as our overwatch."

"That's sweet music. So take everyone down with no prisoners and no escapees."

"Those are our orders. We have the findings, so we're clear and good to go in with weapons free just like we rehearsed at Langley."

"Yeehah! We'll come locked and loaded. See you then."

David Hartnet did not return to his house that evening. He called Rachel on his house phone and left a message that he would not be coming home that night. He said that she should stay if she could because he would return early the next morning. With that intelligence, I thought that we would find Hartnet at the warehouse, but he never showed up there. This disappointment aside, our raid was flawless. We did find Delgado at the warehouse with five of his thugs, all armed.

"Delgado, this is Anderson. We have you surrounded. You cannot escape. Have your men drop their weapons. You drop yours. We'll talk." I stood tall and spoke confidently and authoritatively. Delgado stood tall too, with his back straight up like the macho man he was reputed to be. He had his men to impress, after all.

"Señor, you are making a big mistake. You drop your weapons. Manuel, you shoot the helicopter. I'll take out this gringo."

The gang's shooting started almost instantly after Delgado uttered the word 'gringo.' My team returned fire. In less than two minutes, all of Delgado's men were slain. I ducked and rolled forward, shooting Delgado four times in the chest before he hit the ground. I raced up to kick his gun away and felt for signs of life. There were none. The helicopter shone its searchlight all around the area looking for hidden targets.

Sammy called out, "Six down including Delgado. None of ours hit."

"Check out the merchandise in the warehouse quickly. Everyone inside!"

"Whoa, Anderson, I've found chemical weapons, protective clothing, explosives, and timers. The chemical weapons have Syrian markings."

"Bill, call in the weapons of mass destruction team and have them secure the WMD in this warehouse." Bill got on his cell phone and started barking out instructions.

"Sammy, get our Agency cleaners in here to take care of the corpses. Is any of the bodies David Hartnet?"

Sammy shook his head. "No, boss. Hartnet is not here. He couldn't have escaped. He just never showed."

"Damn. Sammy, take charge. I've a couple of calls to make." Sammy took charge immediately.

"You've got it. Dick, Clem, and Rudy cover the WMD. Bill, get me an ETA for the WMD team's arrival."

"Sammy, they're inbound, arriving in five."

"Great. Let's get a leg up on the bodies. Cleaners inbound, arriving in two."

Fortunately, we suffered no casualties. As far as I could see, Delgado and his cohorts were taken by surprise, so none of our targets used his cell phone. Where the hell was David Hartnet? Why had he not shown up? Did we have a leak somewhere? Did Hartnet have a sudden fit of prescience? What about Rachel? I figured she'd be okay in any case, but I wanted to be sure.

I texted Rachel, "RUOK?"

She texted back, "IMOK. RU2?"

"Y. Inform me ASAP when David comes back to the house."

At 5 a.m. she texted, "David has returned. He's taking a long shower after what he had called a hard night's work. David is asking me to join him in the shower. I gotta go now." Then she signed off.

That evening, as if nothing whatsoever had happened to affect David's fortunes, David and Rachel were back at the martini bar where they had met the night before. Their pattern was identical to the previous evening's procession from bar to bar, to the small restaurant and then to his house.

According to Rachel's later account, "We made love all the rest of that day, with brief intervals for showers, rub downs, and catnaps. I became comfortable with David, and he was, I think, entirely smitten and very attentive and gentle as a lover." She paused to gauge my reaction to this candid account.

I played it deadpan and told her, "Please go on."

"David received a disturbing call on his cell phone early the next evening. He seemed alarmed and said he wanted to be alone to discuss a few matters with business associates. So David asked me to take off my heels and take a long walk on the beach in my bare feet. He said he'd catch up with me in five or ten minutes. I did as he asked, taking my purse with my cell phone and the thumb drive with me. I called you to report what was happening."

"I remember. I wasn't pleased with the turn of events. I told you that you might now be in danger because for the first time David had wanted to distance himself from you to take his call. Something wasn't quite right. Did he have information coming that might involve you? As you'll recall, I told you to find a place high up along the beach to stash your thumb drive and to keep walking up the beach to the North at a brisk pace. I told you that I would intercept you as soon as possible."

"I intended to do exactly as you said, but you know what happened next."

In hindsight, I did not have to worry about Hartnet chasing after Rachel in a fury to kill her after hearing from his informant. Just after Rachel had called me, David's entire house suddenly exploded and burned to the ground with him inside it. Rachel heard and then saw the fiery explosion. She called me again and told me what she saw. She did not stop to hide her thumb drive but continued walking north on the beach until I found her.

After frantically searching, I found Rachel high up on the beach by a sand dune. She saw me, and half in shock, she flew into my arms. I held her tight and told her that it was all over now.

"I might have been in the house when it exploded." She was sobbing quietly.

"Yes, darling. But you weren't. I'm so glad, so very glad." What else could I say? I held her close until her trembling stopped. She finally breathed regularly, and we walked for a while on the beach together, my arm around her, her head down or looking out to sea. The sirens sounded and the fire trucks and police surrounded the house with flashing lights and spotlights. People came out of nowhere to watch the blaze. After that, we returned to our motel room.

While Rachel showered and changed, I left to buy a bottle of excellent wine. When I returned, she was dressed in her jeans and T-shirt. We drank wine out of the motel's plastic cups while I debriefed her.

The paper cup shook as she held it and she nodded and blinked her eyes, reliving the moment of the explosion.

"I have no idea why the explosion happened. We made love. He told me to leave. I left. I looked back at the house. And bang."

"Rachel, David had been dealing with some very hard men. Those men killed him, but I don't know why."

At this, Rachel became enraged and accusatory. In a harsh voice she fulminated, "You do know why. Your people knew. You had staked him out and watched him. You knew where to find him so I could ensnare him. Tell me. Tell me now."

"Rachel, you'll have to trust me that I did not know that they were planning to kill David. You've done commendable work."

Rachel calmed down. Her shoulders fell. She looked down, trying not to cry.

"Look here, I brought the cash that I promised you. I'm going to count it and give it to you, and then I want you to count it to be sure."

"Thank you. I'm grateful. Thank you for the opportunity. Perhaps I've been unfair. We only met a few days ago, but now I feel that I've known you all my life. I had nothing better to do with myself than to work with you."

We drank wine for a while without discussing anything. I finally set my cup down.

"If you want to work with me in the future, we have to discuss a few details about this first mission. Many things about my work seem disconnected from everything that normal people would expect. Some things happen for no apparent reason. Other things that are important crop up suddenly and no one could have predicted that they would have any importance, but they do. The feeling you experienced when you saw the house blow up with David Hartnet inside it is not aberrant but typical. When you work with me, your life will be in danger constantly. You were lucky on this occasion, but you might not be lucky later. I can't make the danger go away completely. You'll have to take the risk that you might die or be harmed. In this case, David inadvertently saved you from death, not me. I had no way of saving you if David had not told you to walk. You might have died if you had refused to leave him."

Rachel looked into my eyes, and as the choirs of angels sang in my ears, she rose and kissed me gently on my lips. I rose and hugged her close and kissed her hard. Then I held her arms and told her that we were going to get back to this, but first I had some other things to say. We sat back down.

"Please describe for me in as great detail as your memory permits everything that you and David did from the moment you walked up to the bar and got his attention."

"Everything?"

"Yes, tell me everything, every single detail that you remember. Every ordinary action, every intimate action, every name of a place or a drink or a person. Tell me what you did when you searched his house. Take me everywhere you went, and let me look over your shoulder as you go there."

Rachel did that, and I elicited details by questioning what she did not directly say. Her account was remarkable because she remembered everything. She remembered the names of each of the bars and restaurants they had visited. She remembered the names of the people David Hartnet had addressed. She remembered having taken calls, their time and the number of minutes that they took. She remembered details of what David had said and what the other parties had said. She remembered every detail of David's house, and she took me through each room with such vivid descriptions that I felt I had been there myself when she was through. She did not have to strain to recall details. As I looked over her shoulder, she directed my attention to things I might not have seen if I had been there. Her memory was so prodigious, I wondered how it had been trained and what had happened to make her appear ragged on a street corner for me to meet her.

"Rachel, you're like Kipling's Kim with your prodigious memory and discernment."

She smiled and cocked her head at me without making a statement. She was at that moment an enigma. When I asked her what other files were on David's laptop computer besides the files she copied to his thumb drive, she named every file in the order that she had opened them. She had found printouts from some of his files and remembered which files they came from and what their contents were. Rachel remembered that she saw in David's bathroom a single long blonde hair matching another long blonde hair that had lain on the pillow of his bed when he first took her to it. A third such blonde hair lay on the lapel of one of David's suits in his closet. These three hairs went into her purse—and she fetched and showed them to me.

"As for lovemaking, David was experienced but distracted. He seemed to like me well enough, but he was never focused on me enough to take full advantage of what I had to offer. I had to do some very extraordinary things to get David's attention. He had no gift for curiosity or for passion. David was fastidious about being clean, and that was good for me. David was not the world's best kisser, and

I had to be careful when I led in anything that I didn't bruise his ego." At this, Rachel shook her head and laughed.

"Why are you laughing?"

"I took him past all limits he had set for himself. He said so. In the end, David had a great imagination but no daring. He didn't have the courage to persevere."

Now Rachel was looking at me with a stare that I later recognized as her signature. She was daring me to be worthy of the perfect male in her imagination.

"Are you the one?" That was the expression in her flashing black eyes, their pupils dilated to the point where they seemed to swell beyond their natural limits. In a silent conversation, Rachel said, "I want to devour your insides with the power of my eyes."

My eyes silently said, "You are becoming better and better as a prospect with every word that comes from your ruby mouth."

Her eyes looked at me expectantly: "The next move is yours. So go ahead and make it. I'm waiting."

I made the move, went to her and lifted her from her seat to the bed in a single motion. Then I lay beside her and kissed her hard on the mouth. She responded, and for a while we explored each other, fully clothed, with our hands. Her challenge about hand language needed a response, so I rose to meet her challenge, and she saw me rise and smiled. We had no trouble removing each other's clothing piece by piece, lingering to trace a finger here or there.

We wanted to savor each other and to see our effects in a raised brow, a faraway gaze, a look of fierce intensity or daring, a yearning or a triumph. We kissed long and arduously, and then we moved together in a rhythm that I established and she answered. We hugged each other as we moved together and then almost apart and then together again. We now agreed without a word to press to the summit, and we drove and retreated almost and drove again, and inside we had a dialog of softer parts rubbing together. Her eyes dilated and her mouth opened just as inside I felt her open wide, and I knew she was coming when she began involuntarily squeezing and throbbing deep inside and all along me.

"Ooooh. Ahhh, Nghhh, Yes!" she moaned and pressed up against me insistently.

"Mmmmm." I groaned and thrust downward into her as my back arched upwards.

She came, and her eyes asked me to join her. Not yet, my eyes replied because I wanted to push her beyond her expectations. She was delighted to be taken where she had never been, and we left our base camp and pressed for the summit together.

We held like a wax figure composed of arms and legs in contraposition, writhing within a narrow pass and spending energies that flowed from one part to the other.

My eyes said, "Come with me," and we worked slowly to build up our rhythm now that we were one being so that we could together rejoice. She arched and came. I arched and, answering, came also, and came again. And she came again. Both smiling, we knew we had broken through all barriers and achieved what we had intended.

So now the game took another turn, and we descended slowly, not pulling apart but gently as we came down and she trembled slightly and shivered. I juddered and shuddered and called her name, "Rachel." And she said, "Yes." Again she said, "Yes." Was she acknowledging her given name? Was she talking to her soul in a dialog that I only half heard? Her eyes said that she and I were one. I tried to answer her with my gaze. Then I fell upon her and held her. Finally, I slipped to her side. We smelled now like musk and sweat and sweetness. Her hand fluttered over my side. My hand caressed her breast. We kissed sweetly. Then we slept.

In the morning, the Southern California sunlight peeked through a crack in our curtains to reveal us tangled in our wet sheets. We stirred after a profound rest. Rachel rose on one arm, her raven black hair tumbling on my face.

Rachel said, "I had a good time last night. Looks like it's morning now. Want to get up yet?" We decided that we were famished and needed to eat and drink.

When we had both dressed and she was drying her hair with the motel hair dryer, I told Rachel, "I've arranged for you to stay in the motel as long as you like. You're on my payroll now, so you don't have to worry about your expenses."

She laughed and asked, "Does that mean I'm your mistress?"

"I don't care what you call our relationship. As far as I know, neither of us has spouses or fiancés. Besides, I have another important mission for you, and it's going to take some coordination. Are you in or out?"

She smiled her crooked smile, crossed her legs and said, "I am all the way in. Until I am out, that is." I smiled appreciatively. "I'll let you know as we go. So far, we are good to go, Anderson. That is your real name?" I shrugged and looked doubtful. "Oh, then it is like Rachel, a name someone gave you. Hmmm."

Rachel Attains Nirvana

The Agency wanted to give me a commendation for interdicting a nasty threat involving chemical weapons right down in the warehouse district of San Pedro, California. Many heads were on the block for that escapade. Nearly everyone had missed the fact that a whole cache of formerly Syrian chemical weapons had somehow crossed the U.S. border somewhere and went undetected. They remained undetected until I called in the raid on the warehouse, taking out Delgado and his thugs with no casualties on our side. That action opened the door so that our Federal Emergency Management Administration weapons of mass destruction experts could take control of the chemicals and put them in a secure place where terrorists could not get them. Of course in the Agency, as in every other U.S. government organization, no good deed goes unpunished. So now, the most indolent and incompetent people wanted to know how I knew that the chemical weapons were at the warehouse and why I had not informed the proper agencies before moving in to seize them. They did not appreciate cowboy warfare like my rogue, cowboy-style operations any more than they liked chemical weapons.

I told my boss, the Deputy Director for Operations, a brilliant but hopelessly micromanaging harridan no one wants to cross, that in this case, the problem was easy to deal with. Just have the President of the United States give the Director of the CIA a medal and say that on a routine raid of a known terrorist's warehouse compartment, weapons of mass destruction, specifically chemical weapons, were found and the proper authorities were called in to take care of the matter. To her credit, she ran the solution up the flagpole, everyone saluted, and voila, mess managed.

With all the sound and fury, no one asked who had done what to establish the timing of the raid. That was just as well, because my prize agent, Rachel no-last-name, who was not acknowledged, because in Agency records she did not exist, sat wide-eyed munching on her roast beef sandwich and getting rapid-fire instruction from yours truly on her next assignment. I called the assignment "get the blonde" because we were busting ass to find the sometime lover of the man who had died in a blast that took out his home, and almost, but not quite, Rachel with it only one week ago. I did not need and she could not handle the bureaucratic nightmares that daily plague us peons.

"Okay," I said. "DNA analysis indicates that the three hairs you found in the beach house were from a blonde female of Jewish origin with blue eyes and a rare condition—an excessively healthy sex drive." Anderson paused, staring at Rachel expectantly.

"Come on, Rachel, you're supposed to smile when I make a joke."

"When you make a joke, I will laugh." Rachel was clearly amused but tried not to show it because she was eager to get straight to business. "What else do we know about our blonde from your other sources?"

"The most compelling evidence is the picture gallery that you provided us on the thumb drive. Of the fifty-two pictures you harvested, eighteen were of women, and nine were blondes. I had our support team run the images through our facial recognition database, and we hit eighteen for eighteen on positive identification of facial features and eight of nine on the blondes."

Rachel looked down at the floor, her lips pursed in concentration. "So one of the blondes was not a blonde in the picture?"

"Very good, Rachel! For that, you get a latte after you finish your sandwich."

Rachel smiled and batted her eyes yet pressed on. "And have you a profile of the figures you ran through the database? Are they all agents? Or terrorists? Or what?"

"We found a mix of agents and terrorists, with a few that could be either or both. Our non-blonde blonde is one of the ambiguous people. She was working for Mossad, but she disappeared. Some of our analysts who track such things thought she went rogue or maybe went clandestine on a special project that the Institute could not acknowledge. We asked Mossad politely for a sample of her DNA, and they went ballistic. Their director called our director. Asses were chewed. Letters of reprimand went into certain files. The cretins rejoiced. I rejoiced but not for the same reason."

"So will you tell me why you were rejoicing?"

"Why did I rejoice? I rejoiced because the Mossad would not have made this an international brouhaha unless we had found the right target. So bingo, Rachel, we know who we are after."

"Just how far have you been able to narrow all this down to something useful?" Rachel was sitting up in anticipation.

"All right, we have a strong likelihood that the person we are after is one Ruth Blomfeld, not her real name. So what's new? Her last known location was Los Angeles, California, and we are running her mug through the Federal Emergency Management Administration databases now to get a trail on her and a fix. The risk for her is that she could be endangered because the Administration is riddled with spies and informants. The risk for us is that she could be eliminated for convenience before we locate her."

"So how do I fit into the picture, Anderson? I do not see a play for, as you say, 'a beautiful snare' yet."

"Rachel, have a little faith. Ruth Blomfeld has a history, and you have to know it because she is our prey. I don't know how this fits yet, but some years ago an Iraqi agent went into the departure terminal of Los Angeles International Airlines. Without breaking stride, he pulled a silenced weapon and shot an airline ticket agent in the forehead at point-blank range. Airport security pursued him back to his car and shot him dead."

Rachel was now yawning with her fist in her mouth. Her eyes were glazing over. Suddenly becoming aware that Anderson was watching her carefully, she began to draw circles with both hands in the air. The woman was acting like the hopelessly drifting teenager wanting her teacher to get to the point by baiting him constantly.

"I know this seems boring to you, so I will cut to the chase. The airline was the Jewish El Al. The ticket agent, herself a Mossad agent, was believed to be the elder sister of another Mossad agent sometimes known as—you guessed it!—Ruth Blomfeld. Sister or not, Ruth Blomfeld made it her mission in life to get to the bottom of her sister's murder. She did this with the blessing of the Mossad, which never did like anyone killing one of their agents. Anyway, the trail of corpses that resulted from her 'rogue' inquiry included four Iraqi intelligence officers, one female Mossad agent, and one low-level female American diplomat. Our analysis connected all the victims to the hit at the LA airport after the fact. If we had been a little smarter, we might have been able to anticipate each hit in turn. It turned out that we liked the fact that Ruth Blomfeld was doing our dirty work for us."

Rachel looked more animated because the character named Ruth Blomfeld was becoming increasingly real for her. She was trying hard to connect the dots. "So how does this play with the explosion that almost ended my working for you forever, Anderson? Our target is clearly an assassin. She is also clearly a woman who can get in close to a man or woman and kill, then get away clean. Where does that leave us?"

"Let me introduce you to a third member of, let us say, the Blomfeld family, Ryan Blomfeld. Here is his picture. Handsome fellow, don't you think? He is possibly the brother, also Mossad, also blonde, also an assassin. Some think he was the assassin who actually killed the two females for his sister Ruth Blomfeld. No one believes that Ruth Blomfeld was a lesbian, but such things are possible."

Rachel was clearly both disgusted and skeptical. She recrossed her legs and fidgeted in her seat. She got that 'Dare you!' look that was becoming her signature.

"Don't look at me like that. Okay, let's just say that this Ryan Blomfeld is right now all we have to go on. He lives right here in LA and sent flowers to his sister's funeral and gave a moving eulogy for her. In fact, he really likes picking up beautiful women just like you. He doesn't haunt street corners with his Jag like me, but close enough. More like your last target where all we did was dress, point and engage." I wanted her to feel comfortable with the idea, but from her puzzled expression, I felt she needed further clarification.

She forced the clarification by using humor and sarcasm. "So let me translate what you said for both of us. You'll find out where this man Ryan Blomfeld's watering hole is, take me there looking like a billion shekels and send me right into his arms. What am I to say, 'Do you want to buy some Israeli bonds?' or 'Take me home because I am the kind of gentile girl you like to screw?'"

I was confused by her outburst. Now I needed the clarification. "Rachel, something tells me you don't like the looks of Ryan Blomfeld. What gives?"

"Anderson, it is hard to tell what a man is like from his picture. This man looks intelligent, but he is ferocious too. Look at those beady, steel-gray eyes. I can feel him undressing me right here. Yes, I think I can seduce him for you. What then? What do you need from him?"

"Rachel, you will not know what is there until you get inside to know him intimately. When you get that close, count on it, the Mossad will do a thorough background check on you. They will shred your background and try to see any angle by which you have been sent by the opposition to kill him or his sister or both. Once you get inside, I may not be able to get you out again."

Rachel was yawning again. She affected boredom but could hardly sit still.

"It will be for you as if you are inside that beach house waiting for the explosion."

I paused to let this thought sink in. She was fully alert now, and her eyes shone with excitement.

"I hate to put you in this situation, but anyone I send in who has a file in the agency I work for will be identified by one of the Mossad moles in the organization."

I needed feedback, and so far I was not getting what I wanted from Rachel. "If you have a problem with this setup, let me know now." I leaned back and prepared to wait for her answer, unsure how she would respond.

I did not have long to muse, though. She suddenly looked me directly in the eyes and gave her answer right away, with no hesitation in her voice. "Anderson, I have no problem with the setup. I have no problem with making hot passionate love with this man Ryan Blomfeld, who I never knew about until today and I have never met. I do have a problem with you always thinking I am a little girl who will die of fright. I was not afraid of you with your scruffy beard when I climbed into your Jag, was I?"

I defensively ran my right hand over my face, wondering whether the three-day growth was still fashionable. Now that Rachel had put the shoe on the other foot, I had to take new stock of the situation. I must have looked somewhat bewildered now and tried to cover my alarmed expression to mask my anxiety. The woman was approaching from an odd angle, and I did not know where this conversation was leading. She must have read my mind.

"Don't look at me that way. Don't be protective of what you cannot understand. As for my background, let the Mossad geeks try to find out who and what I am. They'll find nothing. Then what will we do? Finding nothing, they will think that I really am a plant because no one can be erased from the record who does not have a record in the database. Better by far that we have a story that can be tested and found to be true. With that story, I'd be safe. What do you think?" Now she paused and measured me with her glittering eyes, which narrowed with a squint of inquiry. She was challenging me, and I knew it. In a flash of insight, I thought she was doing to me what I always did to my boss; So this is what my boss thinks when I maneuver her into a corner!

I told Rachel, "So the best story is the simple truth, but that will not be believed unless it is discovered after piercing through at least one cover story that has some minor flaw. Interrogation, particularly implemented interrogation, is designed to break through false layers one by one until the truth is known."

Rachel was trying to follow my rapid-fire narrative, but I was excited and neglected to give her the opportunity to reflect on what I said.

"Oh yes, you do not know the technical jargon. Implemented means that they inject you with a truth serum-like sodium pentothal. Such drugs affect your brain, and you will say things that your inhibitions or training would prohibit you from saying."

Rachel seemed not to be shocked at all by the thought of being tortured or forced to tell the truth. Yet her growing curiosity about me was irrepressible. She looked down for a moment and then raised her head and focused on me intensely.

"So if I were to drug you, Anderson, I could question you and find out who you really are, what you have done for your agency and whether you really like sleeping with me?" She had a point, about the effects of the drug, but was she serious about using it on me? I decided to turn the tables on her.

"Rachel, some people say that if the right truth serum is used, no one can withstand its effects. I could turn this logic on you and discover who you really are and whether you are actually faking all those orgasms to pet my ego and get something out of me . . . like a latte after sex. Touché?

"Anderson, I am very touched to know that you so value your ego that you would interrogate me with drugs to find out if I am faking when we have sex." Rachel's face was contorted with disdain and scorn for my doubting her sincerity while sharing sex. I tried to look apologetic and forlorn, but she must have read my expression as meaning, 'Well, were you faking or not?'

"I will tell you that you will know when I am faking well enough. With you I do not fake because you are like a truth drug for me. Good sex is better than any drug for opening up the secret compartments of the mind." I was touched by her logic and saw its application at once.

"So, Rachel, you have given the rationale for your seeing Ryan Blomfeld better than I could ever have done. Will you be ready to meet him looking like the zillion-shekel woman tonight at 8 p.m. at the Blue Anaconda bar? That's where the man will be, and he will be alone waiting—for you. He does not know that yet. When he sees you, he will think that he has been waiting all his life for this one moment. The shofars will blow and all his stony walls will tumble down."

"Anderson, I think you may be a rabbi. You know your Testament. It's a good thing you bought me that new blue chiffon dress with the blue heels and the topaz jewelry. I thought you bought them because you were beginning to like me a little. Now I know they are only stage costumes so that my mark will be infatuated with me on sight." Rachel rapidly changed her bearing from amused detachment to vicious satire of herself and me as well. Her eyes were on fire, and they burned into her keeper's soul.

I acutely felt the pain these observations were intended to inflict. Then gradually Rachel's expression softened, and she turned her focus inward and became first intimate, then vulnerable and finally outrageously playful.

"I shall not disappoint you. After this mission is over, I want to see whether we can best our record for orgasms. How many times did we say we achieved them last time?"

"Rachel, the last time never counts anyway."

My becoming the philosopher always engaged Rachel. Again, she was attentive and interested in what I had to say when I shifted onto enigmatical ground. Flippant as she seemed, she always wanted to cut through ambiguity to the core truth, no matter how it hurt her or anyone else.

"Rachel, I promise you that if we succeed in this mission, I will see that you attain Nirvana. Also, I will pay you twenty-thousand dollars, cash. If all you want is the cash, okay, no Nirvana!"

Rachel twisted in her seat and arched back her neck as if drawn by an unseen rope around her neck. She was wrestling with the complexity of my artificial dichotomy. Perhaps if Nirvana was really in the mix, money might not matter after all for her. How could that be?

"You want Nirvana?"

Rachel's expression indicated that she wanted that more than anything in the world, but she would not admit to it. I noticed that her fists were tightly clenched as if she were reliving some recent experience. Her expressions changed so rapidly that I could not interpret which of them to trust. Seeing a flash of her look when she had her last orgasm with me, I thought I had received an answer.

"Yes!" she stated vigorously, biting her lower lip and displaying her irresistible, slanted smile. I could barely restrain my excitement, and return our conversation to business.

"Okay, then. Let's get ready for tonight."

When we were ready to party, I drove Rachel to the bar that would be the setting for her next appearance.

Bars come and go in LA, intriguing the lounge lizards for a year or so and then becoming stale. The lizards slither to the next favored venue and the next. The Blue Anaconda had survived for five years running, and the lizards still played there. Around the outside of the building slithered a giant blue neon anaconda that seemed to strangle the round building upon which it preyed. Inside the lights were low, the music loud and the clientele bored to extinction. Ennui was always in vogue in the early hours of a Friday night.

Everyone inside sat or stood waiting for something to walk up and change the world, if only for a moment. When Rachel walked up to Ryan, I could see the change occur. It was as if Rachel in her lounge regalia had ushered in a general resurrection of the dead. Ryan Blomfeld, the Jew, stirred to life from his deathlike state, and centuries of virile ego stood to attention as he reviewed his future prize from head to toe. He did not know how he managed to deserve this treat for his senses, and he began to peel back all her clothes mentally as Rachel predicted that he would. She said only three words to him, and they magically set the man scrambling into motion. His hand rose suddenly.

"Tequila for the lady!" He smiled, swelled, laid his arm on the bar and said, with no irony, "You're not from around here, are you?"

I saw it all from the dark corner I had chosen to survey the scene. Rachel in motion was better than any practiced actor I had ever seen. I was proud, amazed, jealous, excited and alarmed all at once. Rachel was half right in that an agent like her is like a child to a crusty intelligence operative like me. I get paternal. But then I am a lover too. I thought at that moment that I would not mind pushing Ryan Blomfeld's nose into his brain with the back of my hand just after I drove my knee into his groin.

Yet there he stood, laughing at a joke she just told him from the looks of it. She turned her head to the side, seemingly so that he could admire her profile. Now she was blushing at something he said. Her tiny hands rose up to those luscious lips and tried to cover the smile that burst into view. I raised my hand to order another, but then I saw the pair was on the move, so I paid my tab with a generous tip. I followed the soon-to-be lovers like some loping St. Bernard. She was a good girl because she did not look in my direction. Of course, I hated her for it. I had to remind myself that she was on a mission, but her acting was so realistic I was catching the contagion as well as her prey. I simply could not help myself from my insane jealousy and concern for my agent.

Their round of lounges did not stop at four or five. They stayed for a drink at each of a dozen places. Though I bought drinks of my own, I could not afford to swallow lest my game be foiled. They finally had breakfast at sunrise down on the strip. I thought he might just let her find her way after that, but no. He managed to drive her in his blue Mercedes, out to Mulholland to his luxurious bachelor pad with the pool out back and the view looking out over LA, the loneliest city in the world.

I felt right at home as I broke off my surveillance and returned to the motel, where Rachel's underwear hung to dry over the side of the bathtub, and her toiletries ranged like a Stonehenge on the faux marble top area of our sink. I fell sound asleep until a buzzing sounded in my brain. It was not in my brain; it was my cell phone. Judging by the light coming through the windows, it was high noon. It was Rachel calling that she was safe and Ryan was in the shower. But no, now he was calling her to shower with him. She hung up, and I found myself pounding my head on the side table by the bed. It was going to be the kind of day where my jealousy of Ryan fought against my almost desperate need for information.

Once a day Rachel managed to check in with me. Sometimes it was just the simple text "K" but sometimes it was "K RU?" I was alternately the worried father and the jilted lover until I settled down and began to reckon the options and what ifs. *Perhaps*, I thought, *the man is not who we thought he is. Perhaps*, I feared, *he is a terrorist who will beat, rape and murder Rachel. Perhaps*, I dreamed, *he is going to sweep her off her feet and love her so well that she forgets me entirely.* I envisioned the two of them in a Jewish wedding ceremony under the white awning in the synagogue with the cantor intoning or whatever, and afterward all the drinking and dancing. I saw myself as the unbidden guest with the Uzi and the Jag getaway car. Anyway, I began thinking of ways I could eat a human heart—his I mean, not hers. As amusing as the thought was, though, I knew there was work to be done. I pushed aside my violent and satirical thoughts and turned to the matter at hand.

Then it was pay dirt. My Agency team detected searches of all their databases for a woman, first name Rachel, no last name, her description down to the mole on the upper inside of her thigh, her pierced ears, and the place where she had been nicked with a knife she had dropped near her second toe on her left foot. The Mossad was at work checking on Rachel's Agency connections, of which there were absolutely none visible in any of the databases. I knew they would be thorough. They had her DNA signature and searched for a match. They had weighed her hair, and they had done analysis on her fat content. They had done full blood work. Lord, I thought, what next? I asked my team to be sure to gather all the search routines and associations as well as the Internet Protocols or IPs from which the searches were made.

She was checked against all terrorist and suspected terrorists. She was checked against Interpol records, bank records, employment records, hospital records, and police and military records from all countries. She was checked against Mossad and the Federal Security Service of the Russian Federation and European Union Interpol records. They had a Shanghai IP that checked her against Chinese records. They came up with nothing, anywhere.

And now I thought they would be getting very nervous. How could it be that nothing about her matched anything that lay on the public or private Nets? Surely that must mean, those gray men thought, that her records had been erased. Some agency must own her. She could not possibly be a freelancer. Her beauty was so generous that she must have been identified by someone. A screen test? A beauty pageant? A photo in one of the media? Surveillance camera systems? Other searches? Yes. She had been identified in searches, all of those were their searches. I was now in a state of horror that Rachel and my suspicions had been borne out. She would be murdered or interrogated to find the truth. It turned out to be much worse than that, much worse, and I should have seen it coming. I should have guessed.

They decided to have Ryan Blomfeld pleasure the truth out of her. She confirmed this with the simple text, "XTC" and I was driven to near distraction of a jealous rage. How dare they! She must be saved—and now! Those were the thoughts that ran through my apoplectic brain. I calmed myself by resolving that business was business. I breathed deeply and closed my eyes tightly. I paced back and forth in the room like a caged animal. *At least*, I rationalized, *they haven't yet resorted to powerful mind altering drugs and orientation tortures…or…surgical means.* When I pitted what they were likely doing against what might be done, I was somewhat reassured. These were Israelis, not the ISIS maniacs. These men and women would not deliver Rachel's peerless head to me in a sack. I shuddered at the thought.

Finally, Rachel texted that Ryan Blomfeld had been called to Jerusalem for a few days, and she was left to watch his place. Guards watched the exterior, and a maid came once a day to clean. She exercised daily by walking or jogging, always followed by one of the guards. She texted that they might be following her texting letter by letter, but she doubted it because our exchanges were double encrypted. No one had cracked the demon interface—yet. Rachel wrote that she had let them break through to the right story. I knew that we had reached our goal. She was now going to be trusted. I texted that she should keep her eyes open and her wits about her.

Rachel texted "LOL" and I became furious. I slammed my fists on the nearest table and kicked a chair across the room. I was on the point of dropping my cell phone to crush it underfoot. When I peeled myself off the ceiling and calmed down, I wrote, "RUNXTC?"

She wrote, "XX RU?" I texted "XX LTR" and "XX" again. Having learned that Rachel was safe, I redoubled my search for anything that may have emerged from the negative results of the search routines, and I found absolutely nothing. I did not stop there, and it was good that I did not.

My team had continued to track down every connection that led to a shipment of chemical weapons to San Pedro, California. The labels on the chemical weapons had been photographed by my team before the weapons of mass destruction team had taken the weapons away. We had discovered the precise location of the chemical weapons storage facility in Syria from which the weapons had been taken. We traced their numbers from that source through Russian controls to a U.S. Navy ship that was sent to destroy the weapons at sea. We obtained from the Department of Defense the certification that those weapons had been destroyed as directed many months ago. Yet the weapons still ended up in a warehouse in San Pedro. There was no doubt about it. So I began my calculus, and I looked for what could have happened. I was irritated by the confusion and eager to find information and connect the dots.

I reasoned that the weak link in the chain was either on the Syrian side at the facility, on the Russian side in transit, or on the American side in the destruction. The simplest explanation, according to Occam, is most likely. That meant that the weapons had been cloned, and the real weapons had been shipped via a different route while the clones were shipped through the prescribed, official route. That way neither the Russians, nor we Americans, had been responsible for the diversion of the weapons.

If Syria was the perp, then the most likely conduits would have been the Iranian Quds Force and Hezbollah. The latter would have preferred to keep the chemical weapons in their theater to use against Israel. The Iranians were known to be stockpiling weapons of mass destruction to use against U.S. interests at the right moment. Exploding chemical weapons in LA would cause a great panic, particularly if that happened with no warning, and the effect would be multiplied by collateral actions at other locations.

Just finding the substances in San Pedro had caused repercussions in at least a dozen U.S. agencies. Blowing up a house to hide evidence and eliminate a possible insider threat indicated to me that what was happening was larger than a single cache of weapons. The presence of a top Israeli seducer and assassin showed that the Mossad was looking in the same direction as I was. As far as I knew the Mossad had not informed the Agency of any intelligence of any plot against the U.S. To the point, the Jewish State had given no indication of a particular plot on U.S. soil involving weapons of mass destruction. That was a curious omission given the Blomfeld connection. I began to think that I was onto something huge that we had all overlooked. Exasperated by the constant focus on small, unconnected facts, I tried to open my mind and look for paths of analysis I had not already tried.

How did the chemical weapons get from Syria to San Pedro through all the sensors that guarded every access by land and water into the country? I eliminated an approach from Canada for the moment because of highly classified safeguards that existed in Vancouver. I could not exclude Mexico, but the conduits for transiting chemical weapons would involve drug and human trafficking networks that were not equipped to handle the lethal chemicals. That left delivery by sea aboard a container ship, perhaps. And that meant China. I knew from open sources that Chinese banks had served as conduits for Quds Force operational funds. Could China clandestinely be funneling chemical weapons for the Quds Force, either intentionally or unintentionally?

On a hunch, I had my support team do an analysis of how chemical weapons could have been transported from the point of origin by land and sea or air and sea to San Pedro, California. I wanted all container ships for the last three years coming to the Los Angeles ports to be identified and traced to origin with their manifests and routes. On the other side of the world, I asked that the Team trace all shipments of containers originating in Syria to whatever overseas destinations they visited. I also asked that the Team run all those records against the tracks of all ships known to be used or owned or chartered, directly or indirectly, by the Iranian Quds Force and by the North Koreans. I requested that particular attention be paid to those Quds Force ships that were known habitually to have altered their Automated Identification Maritime Systems reporting protocols. Then I had an insight that was truly lateral because it jumped from what I knew—the weapons, to what I must look for next—the source. I had been fixated on a strictly linear, logical analysis, and that had gotten me nowhere. I spent a couple of minutes musing on the patterns that the data suggested. Now I stepped back from the facts and asked what might be missing. The answer hit me like a ton of bricks. I jumped from San Pedro where the chemical weapons had been found, to the movements of the Quds Force, the presumable source of the weapons.

I asked for the Agency liaison folks to poll their contacts in the special forces of the U.S. military about any boardings or attempted boardings of Quds Force ships, with the results of those boardings. I asked them to also poll the Israeli Mossad and Aman about similar boardings, particularly those possibly involving suspected weapons of mass destruction transport.

I knew that by initiating these searches I would stimulate the sleepy watch standers to suspect that something nefarious was going on regarding the weapons. Essentially I was signaling that we had a significant threat action against the US. And the threat was genuine. Did we not find chemical weapons in a San Pedro warehouse? We had not found traces or suspicions; we had found the actual weapons themselves. I was acutely aware that by jostling the Mossad, I was playing with fire. In fact, the fire came right back at me, or rather it came right back at Rachel in the house that looked out on Los Angeles.

I got the crucial text from Rachel only two hours after I had sent my last email asking for the analysis of nautical data. She wrote, "Sis S here! IMOK. Can U come up?"

I thought that I had once again gotten lucky. I texted "Can U come down with Sis?" She texted "Hamburger 4U K?"

I texted "K. CU2 N30?"

She texted "S" and we were set. I arrived at the hamburger joint where I first took Rachel after she jumped from her street corner perch into my Jag. I checked out the surroundings and commandeered our favorite table in the back with the view. Maybe we should watch out for any bacon in our food. Then again, perhaps I was just old fashioned. So I sat and waited, checking my email on my cell phone.

The two women arrived right on time. Rachel brought Ruth to the table and introduced her. By their walking arm-in-arm, and by their laughter in each other's company, they clearly had an understanding, and why not? They were twins in many ways. They were stunningly beautiful, natural spies, highly intelligent, energetic and sexually charged. Ruth was a supernatural blonde and Rachel had raven-black hair. Both women could have been Jewesses. I saw this for the first time when the women were together. I had not even thought about that possibility until now. Looks like I made the right choice, naming my version Rachel. While Rachel bought the food, I got right to the point with Ruth.

"We have a common problem, and its name is chemical weapons." She appraised both me and my words carefully.

She said, "Yes, we have a common problem, but its name is weapons of mass destruction." Her gray-blue eyes glittered. Unstated, but clear nonetheless, she was on a mission, and her mission was now our mission.

"It's good that we decided not to meet today."

She nodded in agreement. "It's also good that we did not choose to talk about things we know nothing about, like explosions at beach homes and raids on warehouses in San Pedro."

I laughed and said, "Ships don't always sail where you want them to."

"It's not the ships but the cargos that are important."

How could I disagree? Fortunately, Rachel brought our lunch at this point.

"Ruth, how's your brother been since we last saw him?"

"He's fine. He's back in the homeland for a while visiting family."

I took a long shot and said, "Speaking of family, I was very sorry about the death of your sister. I wish I could do something to make things better, but I understand that you and your brother had done everything possible."

Rachel might have been on another planet because when Ruth looked at her for a reaction to this, she was a blank slate. Ruth gave me a cold look and said, "I've done absolutely everything that I could do, but I'm always looking for more ways to help the family get over our loss." I saw in her eyes the conviction that had made her such a lethal assassin.

I said, mostly for Rachel's benefit, "I'm looking at a lot of shipping data to see what it might tell us."

Ruth nodded and mentioned, "I've heard about that and I've been looking at a lot of shipping data too. Sometime, we might want to compare our data, when I have enough to share."

I agreed, laughing, and asked, "How can we be in touch with you?" She threw her head back and leaned towards Rachel.

"I'll tell Rachel how to reach me." She placed one hand on Rachel's while watching my eyes. Rachel's body language as she leaned towards the touch indicated that she was a willing conduit. She gave no indication that she minded being touched. Ruth's look became possessive rather than threatening. It was clear to me that she was as smitten with Rachel as her brother had been, perhaps even more so.

We shared pleasantries, and then it was time for the women to return to their nest high on Mulholland Drive. I returned to the motel and my agony. I decided to focus on my nautical tracking, because only a breakthrough would get me together with Ruth again. That was the only way I could ascertain the fate of the hostage in this play who was Rachel. I was anxious but not alarmed by the situation. I resolved to keep drinking while I thought things through.

In the middle of the night the breakthrough came. My team actually deserved the credit for the discovery, and they arrived at it by accident. They saw a pattern in interdictions of Quds Force and North Korean vessels in the Eastern Mediterranean Sea. At least one other interdiction was accomplished by our U.S. Navy SEALS. All interdictions were of relatively small container ships. One vessel had been interdicted, boarded and searched by both Israel and the U.S. That vessel was also known to be a conduit for arms and technicians from North Korea to Syria.

My Team had done an analysis of the movements of that ship over a three-year period. The ship had effectively been a ferry between North Korea and Syria. Its cargo was thought to have been experts, missile technology, nuclear materials, biological weapons and chemical weapon materials. In other words, the unit was a weapons of mass destruction treasure house. It had also transshipped cargo at many ports at which Chinese ships often stopped.

One of my team did some correlating of routes. He discovered that one Chinese ship had eight months before our raid picked up a container labeled "machinery parts" that had been left there by the Quds Force ferry vessel. The Chinese cargo ship had made many other stops prior to entering the Port of Long Beach, where seventeen acres of ground are titularly the property of the People's Republic of China. Long Beach and San Pedro are only a stone's throw away from each other. A container labeled "machinery parts" could be shipped by land without inspection from Long Beach to San Pedro. My team had checked, and they discovered that was exactly what had occurred. We found a transshipped container labeled "machinery parts" that had originated out of the usual channels. In other words, my team now had the smoking gun for the chemical weapons. I could not have been more proud of them for making the connection.

It nagged at me that Ruth had overridden my obsession with chemical weapons to extend the search to weapons of mass destruction generally. To see whether we could make any further correlations, I asked my team to focus hard on the Quds Force ferry container ship to determine what cargo might have been transshipped by Chinese vessels to any U.S. ports. I put an urgent and priority label on this search. I asked that the best analytics folks at the Agency be assigned to assist.

I also called my boss, the Deputy Director of Operations of the CIA, on her secure cell phone. I told her I was tracing a pattern of transshipment of weapons of mass destruction from Syria to many ports in the U.S. I reported that my team had nailed the Quds Force ferry and Chinese transshipment that landed chemical weapons in San Pedro. She shrieked, howled, screeched and complained because she had been totally surprised and outraged by this egregious enemy activity. She said heads would roll because her analysts had failed to discover what I had found. More constructively, she issued the order to expedite and support my team's search, and gave me access to the right Agency experts. That put my team's efforts on a new footing with top-level support within the Agency.

I was now ready to see Ruth again. Rachel had sent me daily texts that all said "K" so I knew that she was all right. I did not know what she and Ruth were doing, but I knew they were doing something that did not elicit "XTC" texts. Anyway, we all met at the hamburger joint again for old times' sake. Burgers, fries, and Cokes were becoming our standard fare.

"Ruth, we've nailed the Quds Force and the Chinese for at least one transshipment of weapons of mass destruction. My Team is now focusing on any and all other possible transshipments."

Ruth was so pleased with this news that she clapped her hands, smiled and said, "I told you so, didn't I? My brother Ryan will be back tomorrow and will relay the news to his family. They'll be happy to see what they can find from their resources based on this new perspective."

"Ruth, I very much appreciate your broadening my views. I was becoming tunneled in my vision. A narrow view was my biggest problem."

"I wholeheartedly agree with you," Ruth said, glad to see her own mission taking constructive form through our growing collaboration.

Rachel also seemed pleased with the turn of events. She said, "I've learned a lot from Ruth up on Mulholland Drive, like how to play chess and do Jewish dances and sing Jewish songs."

I could see that Rachel was about to demonstrate by singing, but that might have derailed our focus on the business at hand.

I said, "I'll hear her you later tonight because you're coming home." I glared at Ruth.

Ruth started to object but then shook her head when she saw the determination in my eyes and agreed that Rachel should do as I said. When we parted, we both hugged Ruth and held her, and then we looked into her eyes and said thanks for everything she had done. We all left the joint together, and Rachel and I watched Ruth skip to her jeep and drive away with screeching tires.

"Ruth is quite the operator, isn't she?" I asked with a smile.

"You don't know the half of it, Anderson. She is one of the great ones in this world." Rachel was infatuated by Ruth. She was beaming with energy just talking about the spy.

"She acts and sounds pretty butch to me." I was taking a blind, intuitive stab here, and I was apparently right on target.

"She is butch, yes, but she sticks with her fellows." Whatever did she mean? Rachel now had a solemn tone.

Startled, Anderson asked, "Whatever do you mean by that? Did she make a pass at you?" I had no idea that the women would be so attracted to each other.

"She knew that I was hetero and that was okay with her."

"I'm much relieved to hear that." In fact, I was overjoyed at this news, and I relaxed a little because of it.

"Her brother is also great. I can personally vouch for his prowess, but you know something?"

"What?"

"You may remember that I wrote you a simple text that said 'XTC'? Well, I lied. Hahaha. I can see you're mad. Honestly, couldn't you tell at the time that I was teasing you? Were you mad? You aren't saying anything. I was just having fun getting your goat."

"Some fun that is. I don't think it's funny at all."

"Sourpuss! So you were angry with me for having ecstasy with another man? Well, shame on you. Let me remind you that when we started this thread of our mission, you promised me something. Do you remember?"

"I don't remember telling you to lie to me."

"Yes, of course, you remember. Something about Nirvana. You said that when this mission was successfully over, you would see that 'Rachel attains Nirvana.' Well, we've had a major breakthrough in this mission. So I intend to have you prove that tonight and for as long as it takes."

I smiled at the idea. She must have recognized my former concern.

She smiled right back at me. "Now you're smiling again. I like that. By the way, I asked Ruth about Nirvana, and the thought inspired her. She told me that if you could deliver Nirvana to me regularly, there would be no limit to what you and I might do together. I think she was jealous that you even promised something like that. She said no one ever even thought enough of her to give her Nirvana. She's jealous—of me. Imagine!"

We both took a moment to let our imaginations run wild. For me, that was not difficult because Rachel was my muse as well as my bed partner.

"So let's get going. If we start from Los Angeles, can Nirvana be far away? You tell me. No, you show me. Remember how my sign said, 'Ride?'"

I nodded, smiling.

"Good. Well then, yes sir, let's ride!"

Rachel Goes the Extra Mile

I had been doing a lot of thinking about Rachel while she was held hostage by the Blomfelds on Mulholland Drive. Some of my thinking was downright unprofessional, I admit, but I had made an investment of money, time and emotion that had paid off any way you looked at it. What bothered me increasingly, though, was not how progressively Rachel was getting under my skin, but how well the scenario we had discussed to insinuate ourselves inside the Mossad operation had worked.

Why was I bothered about what had apparently worked? Well, when I had postulated that Rachel was entirely off the grid, I also figured that Mossad would think that anyone who was found to be entirely off the grid had to have been purposely erased from it. Rachel and I rightly considered that we would need a cover story to account for such an erasure, and the cover story had worked. What I did not consider until recently were the implications for me that Rachel actually was found to be off the grid. No doubt, I reasoned, all evidence of Rachel's prior existence had to have been erased by an agency. No other rationale worked.

I was nervous that my ad hoc agent could be a spy. Eventually, I would have to ask Rachel about her past, but right now we were on a roll. I decided to defer my intrusive questions about Rachel's past until a suitable occasion presented itself.

Meanwhile, I counted out her latest pay for services—twenty-thousand dollars in cash, and I handed the pile of hundred dollar bills to her across the table at the motel. She accepted the money without hesitation, a satisfied smile lighting up her face. With a purr, she said that she had genuinely achieved Nirvana. I was pleased because she had achieved Nirvana with me and not one of our targets. We were both doing very well in our relationship together, and things were just getting off the ground with our operation.

This morning my team gave me the latest news about the people in the photographs Rachel had downloaded from the laptop at the beach house. Predictive analytic algorithms had discovered that the men and women pictured in that cache, taken together, would be either the best weapons of mass destruction terrorist outfit or the best weapons of mass destruction counterterrorist outfit in the world. I thought they were a mix of the two. They were hard to sort out because counterterrorists often had to infiltrate terrorist cells to be effective and terrorists had to infiltrate counterterrorist cells to avoid being eliminated. Take, for example, the case of Mossad agent Ruth Blomfeld.

Rachel's time on Mulholland Drive had allowed her to get to know Ruth Blomfeld like the sister whom Ruth had lost. Ruth's being bisexual made their relationship complex and potentially explosive. Rachel remained coolly objective about Ruth on one level, but on another level she genuinely liked the Mossad counterterrorist and assassin. Coming down from the mountain was an ambivalent experience for Rachel, especially since Ruth's brother was just about to return from Jerusalem where he had conferred with his people at Mossad Headquarters. Rachel rationalized that she could always return to the Blomfelds if need be. Meanwhile, she was gaining valuable perspectives on her mission from working with my team here at the motel and with me.

"So you have evidence that weapons of mass destruction have been transshipped from the Middle East to major ports within the U.S." She made this declaration deadpan but raised her eyebrows skeptically.

"Incontrovertibly, yes, we do."

"Do you have evidence of who is coordinating these transshipments or when those weapons will be employed?"

"Not yet," I admitted, eyes downcast.

"No? Do we have any guesses?" Rachel always hit the nerve. I glared at her accusatory tone and looked away, refusing to make further eye contact.

"Look, Rachel, Agency experts, are working hard on unlocking every scenario to get to the bottom of those mysteries. My best guess is that the General of the Quds Force is the operational coordinator for the terrorist mission."

"Is that because the Iranians like a strong commander who micromanages things from the top?"

"That's true, but there's more. The assets he controls are Iranian cargo ships, some of them flying false flags. As for which nation state is directing traffic on a higher level, you can choose one or more, or all, of the usual suspects: Russia, China, Iran, Syria and North Korea."

Rachel considered this. I could tell that she understood the scope of what I was saying. She bit her lower lip and focused hard while she listened.

"So we are looking at significant threats to security behind all this?"

"We have no proof. The way the most secretive and lethal terrorist organizations worked, nation states had to be involved behind the scenes. Those nations nonetheless needed to be perceived as being unconnected from the terrorists. Proof of their involvement usually did not result in open accusations but in quiet diplomatic negotiations to desist. The idea of not negotiating with terrorists made sense since no one negotiated with the terrorists. Negotiations were done with those who funded and protected the terrorists."

"So we are looking for needles in haystacks? I hope all those computers and experts are as good as you think they are. You told me a few minutes ago that you found chemical weapons in a warehouse in San Pedro. So what was the terrorists' plan to use those weapons? Can you guess when and how they planned to use them?"

My mournful frustration told her the answer.

"No?"

"In a word, no!"

"When you have no answers, you should fall back on what you know. So when do we get to break our own record for orgasms?" Rachel ran her bare foot up and down my calf, twisting a lock of her hair in her fingers. With a smirk, she pinned the hair above her mouth in the form of a mustache. She had unique ways of being silly and sensual at the same time, and I loved her for it.

We laughed, and I rose to tickle her and one thing led to another, and another. We had no trouble navigating to the bedroom while casting off our clothes in all directions.

Rachel was correct about two things. We could break our record if we tried. And it is best for people who are stuck on a problem to open up the possibilities by having wild, glorious sex with a ravenous goddess. How boring an ordinary office would have been for our deliberations! Now that I think about it, if our government allowed anytime sex, the productivity of our agencies would skyrocket. Communal office showers would also be good. I reflected that the old biddies in Agency Human Resources would go apoplectic over the very idea.

What occurred to me after Nirvana II was the criticality of variegated weapons of mass destruction implants to a single grand plan. Any of the weapons detonated in isolation would have only limited effects, though, to be sure, terror would be a significant effect. To get above the tactical level to the strategic level, the various weapons of mass destruction would have to explode simultaneously or at least in a sequence that created the conviction that nothing was safe.

I had devised an exercise for the U.S. Northern Command on that premise using a mix of chemical, biological and radiological weapons at locations on the east and west coasts, and the exercise created pandemonium. Because I could design and execute an activity like that, so could a master terrorist. The only difference was that I could make assumptions about the locations of the weapons without having to take the time and labor to get the actual weapons in place.

In the exercise, I used our sensor arrays against the national plans by presenting false targets to divert critical defensive assets from real weapons in other areas. The military officers who ran the exercise never could catch up with evolving events, but I doubt if any lessons were actually learned. Maximum confusion would be the result of a real-life scenario. That is why my team and I had to get out in front of the action. The San Pedro chemical weapons were the tip of a very nasty iceberg, at least in my mind.

Rachel emerged from the steamy motel bathroom wrapped in towels as she always did. She sat down opposite me looking bright and clean, radiant and triumphant. She put her feet up on the bed and her towel slipped, revealing a glimpse of her peaches-and-cream complexion all the way up her exquisitely shaped thighs. Magnificent! I told her to go and get dressed or we would lose the entire afternoon. She feigned a pout and went back into the bathroom to put herself together and get dressed.

Meanwhile, I got my team on the line to discuss how we might game the terrorists' timing strategy.

"We should start with the premise that the chemical weapons cache was one piece in a large puzzle-like operation. Major ports would necessarily be involved in such an operation; New York-New Jersey, Chicago, Boston, Galveston and Los Angeles. I want you to draw up a plan as if you were terrorists. Identify the materials and weapons the terrorists would need to cause chaos. Use our major ports as a starting point. Ask how the terrorists might get their weapons to facilities in or near those ports. Use the methods used to install the chemical weapons in San Pedro as a model. Match plans to actual ship movements and transshipments to revise the notional plan to match reality."

Simultaneously, I challenged my team, "Think harder about how the men and women whose photographs we harvested could fit into one grand plan." I did not know what my team would find, but the activity would get their minds working on the big picture.

Rachel emerged from the bathroom and plugged her hair dryer into the wall by our makeshift command table.

Before she turned the hair dryer on, she said that something had occurred to her during our coitus. "It might be nothing important," she said, "but have any forensics been done on the beach house that exploded?"

"What are you suggesting, radiant goddess of the bath towel and hair dryer?"

Rachel held her hair blower like a scepter as she thought how she could narrow her idea without losing it. "Specifically, was a body found in the wreckage? If it was, has a DNA analysis been done on it?" Then with a flourish she turned on that infernal machine and became lost in her mechanical task.

I had to dash outside into the brilliant Los Angeles sunshine to make the frantic call to our forensics team. *Why had I not thought of that? Why had she? Maybe there was something to her Nirvana thing after all.*

Agency forensics told me that one body had been found in the smoldering wreckage of the beach house. It had been burned beyond any recognition by the fire. No DNA analysis had been done because the LA Police Department had assumed that the lone body belonged to David Hartnet, the owner of the house, and what was left of the body had been cremated. No DNA analysis was possible now. I was furious because the man who had collected the photos in that laptop would have been critical to the coordination of the strategic terrorist mission. My belated insight, stimulated by Rachel's innocent query struck like a thunderbolt, *What if the beach house explosion had been part of a plan to allow its owner to disappear so that he could continue to coordinate the activities of the terrorists without being watched?*

The more I considered this theory, the more it made sense to me. Why had the man not appeared at the warehouse? Why had he asked Rachel to take a walk on the beach when he was talking on his cell phone? Why had he left the laptop without any encryption or password protection where Rachel could find it and copy files from it? Who was the man David Hartnet anyway? If he had faked his own death, he had also casually allowed a significant portion of his operation to be taken out. Could it be that our finding the chemical weapons and taking out the connecting team to the terrorists was all meant as a diversion?

I went back into the motel room and found the goddess writing notes furiously on a document in the laptop that I had given her. When I tried to interrupt, she raised a hand to stop me in my tracks while she kept her head down looking at her screen. I went to my laptop at the other side of the table and began writing too. I wanted to get my questions lined up and prioritized so that we could go over them together. She finished before I did.

Rachel said, "There was no DNA check, right? But there was a body found, right?"

"Right and right! You hit the nail on the head asking about the DNA analysis." I was very proud of her for suggesting the idea.

"And no one knows whose body that was because everyone thought the body must belong to David Hartnet, the man who owned the beach house. Typical LA Police Department! Now we cannot be sure that the man we thought was killed is actually dead." I knew she was right. I let her imagination run.

"Okay, now play it forward and what can we deduce?"

"Hartnet's being alive makes sense because only a kingpin of the terrorist operation would have had all those pictures we found in his laptop. So we have to find the man somehow if he is still alive. And it may help to find the name of the man whose body was found in the ashes of the beach house."

"You are an angel!"

I rose and took her in my arms. I hugged and kissed her. We both laughed and she ruffled my hair.

"By the way, I am famished. Angels might live on pure air, but I'm going to order us a pizza."

"Rachel, you can think about eating at a time like this?"

"Of course, dummy you. Girls can't live on sex alone. Pepperoni? Double cheese? Thick crust? I'll phone the order in right now. I hope you're as voraciously hungry as I am."

"Rachel, we have things to think about. Time is of the essence here."

"You know what I am likely to do if I don't get some food right away." She began to unwrap her irresistible body. I was mesmerized by her beauty.

"Don't look at me that way, you lecher! All right, do look at me any way you like, but let's not get started with sex because, as you say, we have brainy lists to make and things to do."

I could not have put things better myself, but then I would not have been bouncing all around the room, shaking my raven mane and waving my arms while looking like Audrey Hepburn on a tirade while in the nude.

The pizza delivery driver took his sweet time arriving at our door. Meanwhile, Rachel got presentable and we compared our voluminous notes. By our third pieces of pizza, we had concocted our plan of attack. The first order of business was arranging a hamburger lunch with the Blomfeld siblings. That was easy. We set the meeting for tomorrow at noon.

Lunch was the first time I got a chance to meet Ruth's brother Ryan Blomfeld, a very handsome man whom I hated on sight because he had sex with Rachel. I restrained myself from strangling him right there, probably because I saw the "touch him and die" look in Ruth's steely blue eyes. Ryan clearly was smitten with Rachel, and Ruth was smitten with her too. As the odd person out and feeling embarrassed being a fourth wheel on a three-wheel vehicle, I decided to take charge. I had a fat chance of that with the three of them unified against me, but out of charity they let me spin my tale and tell the Blomfelds what we would need from the Mossad.

Ryan Blomfeld said, "My sister and I arrived at the same conclusion about David Hartnet independently only two days ago and then only tentatively. We'll share our information as long as you share yours with us."

"Since we are sharing," Rachel asked, "shouldn't we show our good faith by what we found in Hartnet's laptop?"

I replied, "Yes, we can do that. Give them your thumb drive."

Across the table, Rachel handed Ruth her thumb drive with the pictures. Ryan raised an eyebrow and looked at me. I shrugged. Rachel then coolly asked Ruth, woman to woman, to make sure that we got their mug shot collection for this operation in return.

Rachel then turned to me and said, "I'll make some notes to go with the pictures and send them by email to the Blomfelds tonight."

I needed to clarify our mutual position in case either of our agencies got antsy about our rogue arrangement.

"I want to be clear that we never had this conversation. In fact, we never met here or anywhere else, and we shall never meet. Any data we exchange will naturally not be marked with any official markings. It never happened."

Feeling like a Rule Marm, I persisted, "No one in my Agency knows anything about any operational link with Mossad for this undocumented mission. I hope that no one in Mossad except you, Ruth and Ryan, knows anything about an Agency link through me."

The Blomfelds smiled painfully but nodded.

Ruth suggested, "Why don't you send Rachel back to Mulholland Drive to work as your liaison from there?"

I replied with an air of finality, "No. That will be impossible. I need Rachel beside me right now. Instead, she'll serve as a courier for information that is too hot to pass in hamburger joints."

With that decided, we all shook hands on our bargain. We four did know that a handshake was priceless. Our word was our bond. Our mutual hunt for David Hartnet was now unofficially and deniably underway.

Rachel had gone the extra mile in the last forty-eight hours. By going there, she had made a critical difference in our approach. The way she thought and acted with such grace under pressure was my first inkling that she had been through this sort of deep, specialized operation before. Had she formerly been Agency? Was she Agency now? I held back from asking, for now. I did not care that Rachel kept her inmost secrets from me. I only cared that we were set on our mission. We were working far enough off the Agency's reservation that we might actually do some good. In fact, we might catch some terrorists before they struck our nation with weapons of mass destruction in a surprise attack that would make the events of September 11, 2001, pale by comparison.

Rachel and I returned to the motel with renewed purpose. I dashed off at least thirty emails to my team before I felt Rachel's hand on my neck and her hair on my head and her lips on my ear blowing softly.

"Time for bed," she whispered in a way that did not mean, "Time to go to sleep." As usual, we were in agreement, but tonight our sex was not to set another record. Instead we made love slowly, sweetly and thoroughly, and at last we slept the sleep of angels.

Rachel on the Beach

That next morning, I was awakened by the shafts of sunlight that came into the motel room through the small spaces in the window shade. Rachel had already risen, and at the low table by the window she was intently studying the notes that we had made last night. She held a steaming cup of coffee in her left hand while her right worked her keyboard. Her raven black hair was outlined by an aureole of light, and I followed the lines of her legs, one tucked up under her and the other fully extended under the table. I admired her gorgeous body and recalled the pleasure of sex with her. My appreciative eye followed the line that defined her left breast under her tank top.

"Want a cup of coffee?"

"Not just yet." I continued to gaze at her with wonder as if I was transfixed by her beauty. She blushed at the candor of my expression.

"Not yet? Okay, take your time. I have an idea I want to discuss with you. So if you don't want coffee now, maybe we could both wake up by taking a needle-cold shower together."

I frowned at the idea and shivered slightly as if I felt the sting of the cold water just from her mention of it.

"Okay, the needles are out. How about a hot, lathery shower with lots of soap and our hands wandering all over each other?"

I smiled and saw that her invitation was serious. I nodded reflectively.

"I thought so. Race you?"

"Slowly, Rachel. I like to enjoy our time together."

"Okay, take your time. I'll run the water and lather up. Join me when you like."

One of the things I liked most about Rachel was her joy in her own adaptability. She accommodated to your wishes even before you had them. She was the perfect complement to me in all my humors. She genuinely liked our sex, but she was happy to take it whenever we both wanted it. We were always available for each other. Neither was reticent or reserved. We were voracious and passionate standing, sitting, lying, crawling, anyway at all.

If there were Scout merit badges for coital positions, we would have won them all. We had begun designs for the Nirvana badge with stars for subsequent awards. We feared that individual stars would be insufficient to represent what we felt when we were in ecstasy together. I reflected that we were not actually counting orgasms and Nirvana moments anyway. The more we concentrated on numbers and mechanics, the less we soared and wandered to new horizons and summits in the clouds.

In contrast, Rachel never talked about our sex at all. She was either all action or all inchoate, unverbalized suggestion. This was ironic because even when she was absorbed in something having nothing to do with sex, she was sexy doing it. Rachel seemed to be entirely unaware that she could drive me to distraction by a gesture or a subtle shift in her position or with her hand simply sweeping her hair behind her ear.

Our terrarium of the shower compartment was a special place where we left our inhibitions outside the shower door. She was pink and white and rose colored, lathering herself and her hair and letting the hot water channel itself all over her. When I took her in my arms, our wet bodies slid against one another without effort and we laughed with joy. My pulse quickened as I became hard, the motion exciting me more and more. She felt light as a feather as I lifted her with the backs of her knees on the front of my elbows, her legs wide apart on both sides of me. As we kissed, I entered her and her head swung back as she settled down upon me, taking me entirely into her.

I kissed her warm breasts, took one nipple in my mouth and licked it with my tongue. I sucked to harden it and make her throb below against me. She always knew when I was ready, and she watched me carefully as I withheld ejaculation as she rose to the occasion. She quivered deep inside and opened wider than she thought was possible. Her eyes sought mine beseechingly, and then I came as she came, and we both swelled and throbbed together and came again.

Slowly afterward, I let her come down, lowering one foot and then the other until her body, now standing, pressed against mine, her bare feet on top of mine and her mouth greedy for my kisses. Rested and refreshed, we then began to soap each other, each washing every crevice of the other and following every line. At times like this, we knew that on impulse we might begin again at any point. Today Rachel had something important to tell me, so reluctantly we ended our shower and stepped back from our clouds and rain into the warm room where we dressed. She dried her hair with the hair dryer while I made our coffee. We sat across the table from each other, and her foot wandered to rub against my calf under the table while she talked.

"If we approach our search in the wrong way, then we'll never find David Hartnet because he is the needle in the haystack. Two people you know have had intimate knowledge of David Hartnet, Ruth and me. We, two former lovers, should compile separate profiles of the man so that we can exchange the profiles for mutual advantage."

"That makes good sense. Anything else?"

"Yes, I've lots more since you care to hear it. Let's have your Agency Team renew their exploration of the connection of David Hartnet with the Mexican called Delgado. Somehow the Mexican connection might prove significant. As for Hartnet, three things are probable from my knowledge of men. First, David Hartnet is likely still to be in the LA area, though he is probably in disguise. Second, David Hartnet is a lounge lizard so he may be found in one of his usual haunts. Third, David Hartnet likes to make love with beautiful women so he will be susceptible to the same kind of tactics that we used before."

I could find nothing wrong with her logic and agreed. I said, "If the chemical weapons were a red herring, some other form of weapons of mass destruction is likely to be present in the greater LA area. San Diego is also a possibility because of the presence of the Navy fleet there."

"I'm going to task the Nuclear Emergency Support Team to check all port warehouses and container yards from LA south to the Mexican border and all ports from New York-New Jersey to Charleston for any signs of radiological materials. I've already ordered a review of all false positives for biological weapons and chemical weapons at all ports in the U.S. for the last two years. It would be easy to defeat even our most sensitive sensors for signs of those weapons of mass destruction."

As an afterthought, I said, "If David Hartnet was the coordinator of a large, imminent terrorist operation, he would have been doing a lot of traveling to the port areas to visit his terrorist team leaders. We can set up surveillance at the LA nightspots, but we may have to wait a while for our prey to return there. Ironically, the longer we have to wait, the closer the date of the coordinated terrorist attack."

I also told Rachel that the best sensors for detecting David Hartnet in disguise were Rachel's and Ruth's eyes because a woman will always recognize the eyes of a man with whom she has made love. The reverse was not likely to be true, though a man like David Hartnet would recognize either Rachel or Ruth if they appeared with their normal hair color. So for the next month, while they were hunting Hartnet, Rachel became a blonde and Ruth a brunette.

Rachel considered this with a serious look, and then she broke out into a radiant smile. "So now you will have a blonde lover. How do you feel about that?"

I must have positively beamed at her in affirmation.

"I thought so. How typical of men! Is this some kind of trick to make me a blonde for you? Well, I like my raven black hair wherever it grows on me, and so far you have also liked it. When this is over, I will go back to my original hair color, unless being blonde offers advantages." Her smile became suggestive and mischievous. I returned the smile, but there were more important matters at hand.

Going back to business, I said, "I've arranged for our use of an Agency safe house down on the beach. We'll be moving out in the wee hours of tomorrow morning. Our new digs will be much better, with an ocean view and marble in the bathroom, which has butcher-block glass for windows." Rachel said something about our honeymoon being over, but I took her in my arms and said that it was only just beginning.

We moved to the safe house at the beach as I had arranged. I thought that it was great to make a move without having to transfer a van load of belongings. In fact, we fit everything we had in my Jag. Rachel looked ravishing in her excitement about our new adventure, and when she saw the safe house, she was joyful.

"Anderson, it's perfect! Just imagine taking long walks on the beach in the early mornings and late evenings. We can build fires in the dark and watch the sparks fly into the night while we hold each other. We can make love under the stars."

All that was fine with me, but I was now in battle mode. Just before we left the motel, I had received a warning that the Nuclear Emergency Support Team had detected radiological materials at the port of New York-New Jersey. That discovery had put the Federal Emergency Management Administration on full alert, and the Agency wanted to know what specific intelligence I had unearthed to vector the Nuclear Emergency Support Team to make the discovery.

Once again I had to suffer the jealous rage of that harridan the Deputy Director for Operations. Like the Red Queen, she wanted my head for getting ahead of her agenda and hundreds of heads of those who had failed to detect the presence of the weapons earlier. I had to tell the bloodsucking vampire that I had played a hunch based on finding the chemical weapons at San Pedro. She wanted to know how I knew to look for radionuclides, and I told her a few things about asymmetrical attacks until she cut me off, screaming something about keeping her informed of what I was doing. She hung up in the middle of her tirade without giving me a chance to tell her what I thought of her directive.

It's a good thing, I thought, *that the harridan knows absolutely nothing about my operational activities.* As a micromanager, she would want to jump in and interfere however she could. She was all about her own power to control everything in her demesne, such as it was. Instead of power, I was focused on my mission.

I was also focused on Rachel, and she was my greatest secret in my perch off the Agency reservation. I could not imagine what my boss would do to me if she knew about my raven-haired, soon-to-be blonde-haired bombshell. I always thought of Bony Maroni when the Deputy Director for Operations came to mind. Her flaming red hair stuck out in all directions, and her scrawny, bony body angled like pick-up-sticks when she stalked and stormed. Mating with this maniacal princess of the CIA, I thought, would be like mating with a black widow spider, and the male of the human species would end in the same manner as the spider.

My team continued to work their magic while I dealt with the bureaucracy. The dirty bomb materials that the NEST found in New York were novel as well as voluminous. The amount of explosives was enough to equal a low yield nuclear explosion, but the payload for the explosion was more neptunium and strontium and cesium than existed in U.S. stockpiles. The immediate effects of the discovery were ritual firings and demotions from the top right down to the lowly guards at the port facilities. In the agencies, letters of reprimand went out to everyone who was on watch during the period when the weapons of mass destruction had been shipped and stored in New York. My team was unscathed by all the bureaucratic nonsense. I directed them to look for the practical matters of how the radionuclides had been transported and by whom they had been protected on their long journey to their current location.

I received a hot wash report from the National Nuclear Safety Administration indicating that the sources of the materials were Russia and Iran. Wow, what a surprise! Who would have suspected Russia and Iran? My team's back bearings indicated that they had been shipped from Iraq on container ships controlled by the Quds Force. Transshipment was accomplished by a Russian container ship. Our port authorities had turned their heads when remote detection indicated the possible presence of radionuclides among the machinery parts that were listed on the container's manifest. The NEST was not called in to inspect the cargo. Russian-American relations were too valuable back then to do the usual checking. So enough nuclear materials and explosives sat at a warehouse in New York to contaminate the city for thousands of years.

I put together a report on the implications of finding weapons of mass destruction in both San Pedro and NYC, and all I got back from the Deputy Director for Operations was, "This is all wool gathering. Where are the hard facts?"

I figured that I was lucky not to have been terminated with extreme prejudice for daring to cross one of the sacred boundaries between Agency analysts and operators. Operators were not supposed to do any thinking, and analysts were not to do any thinking that was out of the box. Of course, thinking that would protect this country is always out of the box. Policy and bureaucracy can blind people and institutions.

"Well," I told Rachel, "we have to continue doing what we intended fast. The terrorists should know by now that another of their caches had been intercepted."

Of course, the American public knew nothing about the discovery of the radionuclides. It might have eventuated that the CIA would keep a lid on the implications, except that my report for my boss just happened to be posted without attribution as a blog spot on one of the Agency classified blogs. The Deputy Director for Operations threw a hissy fit, but she could not accuse me without seeming to deny the validity of my reasoning, which had gotten the favorable attention of the Director. Of course the Director is a busy man, so it took an email to his Executive Assistant to focus his attention on the blog spot and to tell him how favorably the President would look on an Agency that took the time to think things through and to plan for emergencies. That did the trick.

From our new accommodations on the beach, Rachel and I did a lot of strenuous thinking, frequently punctuated by leisurely runs along the beach, having sex within the sound of the surf and taking long, hot showers together in our marble bath with the enormous Agency towels to dry ourselves afterward.

"Anderson," Rachel said, "I think we must have died and are now in heaven." Her words brought a smile to my face. Shakespeare's Cleopatra, we are told, 'died' many times with Anthony, meaning that she achieved Nirvana repeatedly. She actually lived for a long time, enjoying her sexuality to the fullest while she remained her inimitable shape-changing self until she applied the asp. I shuddered to think what if Rachel should be dead. When I did become morbid, I would hug her tight and look deep into her dark eyes to see the fire of life that played there in the shadows.

It was time for what I later called the Rachel-and-Ruth patrol. Ryan and I would vector the two femmes fatales in bar after bar, waiting for some sign of our prey David Hartnet. Circulating pictures would have been counterproductive, we thought, because we might scare our game away. The women, now a blonde and a brunette, liked dressing up for the kill and visiting the night spots from 10 p.m. until 2 a.m. each night. They were hit on frequently, but they were experienced women who knew how to fend off lounge lizards whom they found repugnant with a cold, disdainful glance.

Ruth had to fend off female suitors as well as males. Ryan knew she was a professional who knew how to protect herself as well as to take note of how to slide a meeting in between the rounds. Sometimes she continued searching in the gay bars until 4 a.m. just to spend time with a lady who had become smitten with this wild brunette. Being off the reservation can have advantages.

At 3 a.m. at the Bivalent Bivalve Den, Ruth hit pay dirt. There at the bar, flirting with a handsome young man was David Hartnet, now a blonde with an unusual tan that Ruth guessed must be a full-body job. She recognized the way he leaned into the bar with his pelvis and the way his hand moved against the cheek of his companion. Ruth drew her brother's attention to the target, and smoothly Ryan became the operator while Ruth became the watcher. This was a maneuver I was not prepared for, but in retrospect it made perfect sense. Ryan, Ruth later explained at the hamburger joint, had always been conflicted until she showed him that he could have his cake and eat it too. In fact, Ryan's swift entry into the fray left the young man confused and alone at the bar as David Hartnet and Ryan

Blomfeld drove off into the early morning sunrise straight to Hartnet's new lair.

The three of us had a celebration lunch the next day at the hamburger joint. Ryan was still with Hartnet, but he had texted Hartnet's address and phone number to Ruth between showers. Ryan was angling for a steady arrangement, but Hartnet was negotiating for a one-night stand. Hartnet was not very comfortable in his new role, but Ryan was an excellent teacher who thought his new pupil showed promise. Ruth was not amused but worried because she knew her brother was in a dangerous situation. Rachel, however, was not in the least inhibited. She smiled to think that Hartnet's sadness after coitus might have had less to do with her inadequacy as a lover and more to do with Hartnet's desire for a male partner.

I was the schoolmaster pragmatist, as always. I wanted to know what the underground elements in the gay community had to do with planting weapons of mass destruction in major ports in the U.S. I recommended that Ryan remain in place as long as possible with David Hartnet. Meanwhile, I told Ruth that I would direct my team to start investigating the LGBT angles of our operation, beginning with our picture gallery. Ruth's eyes narrowed and gleamed dangerously. She was about to explode in fury at this implied slur against the LGBTs. Fortunately, Rachel calmed her by putting her hand on Ruth's arm and smiling her crooked smile.

Ruth melted at her touch and backed down. Some elements in the community, she admitted, had for so long been persecuted that they held grudges. The Mossad had traced some lines of evil involving Shiite terrorists who were gay but would have been summarily killed if the facts were made public. Ruth pursed her lips when she told us that one of her major triumphs had been through blackmailing a Kuwaiti minister, who had confessed to her that he was gay in spite of the fact that the Kuwaiti whom she threatened to inform to was also gay. I asked her to be sure to call for assistance if Ryan found that he was in over his head. Now Ruth laughed, explaining that Ryan positively thrived on dangers of this kind. She said that if a cabal existed among Hartnet's friends and lovers, LGBT or otherwise, Ryan would probe to the bottom of the matter. Now we all laughed, though Ruth was a little perplexed at why we were laughing.

Ryan's daily reports were professional and disturbing. He had been introduced by Hartnet to some very hard gay men who hated America because of what gay people had to suffer. He learned that Delgado had been gay and that a gay network extended down into Mexico along a route that could accommodate trafficking of all kinds, including drugs and humans of both sexes. One weekend Hartnet drove Ryan to San Diego, where they met a tanned and hairless man who walked almost nude each day along the beach at Coronado Island.

The hairless man was known as Vibius. He was the most active bath house figure in the city on the surface. In the underground, he was the kingpin for everything that crossed the Mexican border, both ways. Ryan was introduced as Hartnet's partner, and Vibius invited the pair to join him and some friends for evening bacchanals at a bath house that had survived the bans because it was quietly patronized by gay city officials. Ryan's list of gays whom he met at the bath house was almost as long as the list of medicines he said he would need to take after having had contact with so many people in a single evening. Ryan had taken 1000mg of penicillin beforehand, and he would continue to take that dosage each day, but he thought that some of the participants in their orgy might have tried to infect their partners intentionally. In the pillow talk in a side room off the main bath hall, between the rounds of showers and baths, Ryan had learned that some of the men were furious that Delgado had been so clumsy as to draw attention to the warehouse. What they could not understand was how the New York stash had been discovered. One person said that he hoped the other caches would not be found because the reckoning was drawing nigh. Ryan had not taken the bait because he thought he was being tested. Instead he said, "Hmm." Then to refocus them on sex, he said, "Mmmmm." The sexual play took away need for further conversation about serious matters.

Ryan's text in the early hours of the following morning was disconcerting because of his report of an Iranian-Mexican connection. With no prior announcement, the next day Ryan Blomfeld and David Hartnet were off to Mexico for what turned out to be a week-long sexual odyssey. Ryan's communications became less frequent and briefer. He and Hartnet had been housed at mosques and terrorist training camps whose coordinates were now known through the GPS in Ryan's cell phone. Finally, Ryan was down to "K" and nothing else, and then his communication stopped altogether. Ruth was alarmed at the danger her brother had incurred. She paced back and forth, checking her phone every few minutes.

I told Ruth that the Agency was active south of the border, but we would not want to bring undue attention to Ryan. Hartnet's network would be looking for signs of surveillance by outsiders. We had to wait until Ryan surfaced again before we took any action. If the worst came, I had access to a person who could fly us into Mexico to extract Ryan if he was in extreme danger. As a precaution, I contacted this asset and requested that her Cessna be gassed and ready for immediate takeoff if necessary. I told Ruth the location of the hangar where the plane was kept and to go directly there in case of trouble.

On the fifth day of Ryan's odyssey, Ruth received their agreed signal that Ryan was in trouble and needed our help. He indicated that he might have to use extreme violence to break free and go to ground. Ruth contacted Rachel to say that she was on the way to the hangar, fully armed and ready for assault. I asked Rachel to remain in the safe house to be our command and communication center, and then I grabbed my guns and ammo and raced to the hangar. I called ahead to tell my contact to warm up the plane for us so that there would be no delay. We arrived at the hangar, and Ruth gave me the last coordinates for Ryan, which put him near Rosarita in Baja California. Our pilot reckoned we would fly low over the border going south, but our return would require going farther east than she liked. We were airborne in minutes, and we made the best possible time to a small airport east of Rosarita, which corresponded to Ryan's last known position. We taxied to a halt by the refueling station. While the pilot refueled her plane, Ruth and I scouted the area. Ruth was tense. Increasingly anxious for her brother's safety, she kept checking her cell phone for any signal from Ryan.

As if on cue, we heard gunfire from inside one of the hangars, and Ryan appeared with his back to us. He was running backward and firing into the hangar. We ran to either side of Ryan and took firing positions on the ground. I gestured for Ryan to make a run for our plane, and while he was sprinting across the tarmac, Ruth and I shot dead the four men who were trying to pursue Ryan. We then followed Ryan to our plane, and I told the pilot to finish her fueling and get the plane into the air. Ryan, Ruth and I stood on three sides of the plane to take care of any trouble that might be coming.

"Ryan, what about David Hartnet?" I was concerned about his fate for many reasons.

"The Iranians killed Hartnet because of his failures at San Pedro and New York. They intended to kill me also, but I managed to escape and phone Ruth.'

"So what happened next?"

"With my bare hands I killed one of the Iranian guards and took the man's weapon and ammunition. I held off six others until they charged me. I shot two dead, and the other four took cover. That was when I managed to break for the entrance to the hangar. You and Ruth came just in time to take out my four pursuers." Ryan spoke fast, but his thoughts were coherent. He was, after all, the consummate Mossad field agent.

"Are you sure the seven men you killed are the only ones we need to worry about?" I kept scanning the area for signs of others.

"I think so." He was also looking for possible targets while training his weapon left and right.

I turned to the pilot and said, "I'm going back into the hangar for a minute or two. If any shooting starts, you're to take off with the Blomfelds and leave me behind. I'll find my own way back to the U.S."

I dashed across the tarmac and into the hangar. I knew exactly what I was looking for, and I found it—the body of the Iranian leader of the group that had kept Ryan under fire. Without wasting a second, I took a picture of the man's face with my cell phone. I then found the body of David Hartnet, checked for a pulse and found none, and took his picture as well. With steady hands, I searched Hartnet's body and harvested what I found, including a brace of keys and a folded paper with notes. I heard the airplane cruising just outside the hangar, and I turned and sprinted to it. I leaped aboard the moving aircraft, and it sped to take off just as the Federales arrived with their sirens blazing.

The police did not know what to make of the situation at first. When they found the bodies, they fired at the plane but we were airborne and out of range. The pilot coolly headed for an area she knew that drug runners used well east of Tijuana. We crossed the border so close to the ground that we clipped tall cactus in the process. I made a mental note of how the pilot managed our flight back to San Diego. When we landed, I told her that I would see that she got a bonus in cash for her service. She kissed me on the cheek and turned to look after her plane.

In the air I had sent a text to Rachel, "KKK!" and "XX" and now I wrote a longer text message, "Meet us for hamburgers at the joint." There was no sense doing a hot debrief without the whole team being present to hear it. So we met again at our usual haunt. Rachel walked right up to Ryan and hugged him tight to let him know she was pleased to have him back safely. We ordered our burgers and Cokes and got right to the debrief at our usual table in the back.

Rachel recorded the debrief, but the short version was that Ryan had infiltrated the Mexican-Iranian operation, which was impressive for its infrastructure being just across the border from the U.S.

Ryan said, "The terrorists are coming up from Venezuela through Central America, staging in Mexico and then proceeding to points in the U.S. The terrorists are entirely Iranian Quds Force, and their discipline is impressive. An example of their discipline is the way they questioned and killed David Hartnet." He said this in a hushed voice filled with sadness.

"Tell us how it all went down," I urged him.

"Hartnet tried to shield me by telling the Iranians that I was only along for the ride, but the Iranians wanted to kill me anyway. When Hartnet became heated about my being innocent, the Iranian leader pulled a gun and threatened him. I saw then how vulnerable Hartnet was. I'm very lucky to be alive." Ruth hugged her brother, and we all applauded him.

After our moment of mutual joy, I asked Ryan, "How do the Iranian networks allow the passage of terrorists and materials through the Americas?" This was the crux of the critical intelligence, and I had to know the details.

"The Iranians use Islamic mosques in Mexico as cover for their operation. When David Hartnet reported to the Iranian commander, I heard him tell about the discovery of their activities in San Pedro and New York. He said that Philadelphia and Charleston and Chicago were still on track and that the alternate plan for LA was still in place. That had not been good enough, apparently. The Iranian commander fell into an apoplectic rage before he drew his pistol and shot Hartnet in the temple. It was cold-blooded murder, and the fanatical commander took pleasure from the killing." Ryan gritted his teeth with a look of outrage.

"So why do you think the Iranian killed the lynchpin of the American operations?"

"I believe he thought that the Iranian terrorist mission could probably still be executed, even though two of its primary targets had been removed. Anyway, the Iranian leader eliminated Hartnet because his role had ended." Ryan seemed resigned when describing the savage efficiency of his enemy.

"Now Hartnet is dead and the Iranian leader is dead. What is your sense of the state of play now? Will the plan continue to go forward after the removal of the Iranian leader?" These were Ruth's questions, and they opened the aperture on our mutual mission.

"I just don't know." Ryan was disappointed, but he had no more to contribute at this stage.

I clapped the Mossad agent on the shoulder and smiled at Ruth at the same time.

"You've done outstanding work. You should go back to Mulholland Drive and get some rest."

Ryan retorted, "I first need to wash away my sins and take my medicines." He grinned sheepishly at his sister.

"Ruth, I'll reimburse all your brother's expenses in cash. Please let me know what would be sufficient as recompense."

That evening in the safe house Rachel and I sat side by side, holding hands on the deck overlooking the sea. The moon was full and brilliant, and its reflection was a broken line of silver coins on the undulating sea.

"Anderson, I'm so glad you made it back safely. Ruth told me you went back into the hangar. Apparently you told the pilot to take off without you if they heard gunfire. Mister, I would be very sad if something happened to you." She wept quietly and patted my hand.

"That makes two of us, Rachel," I said, laughing.

She stood and then sat in my lap, looking into my eyes in the darkness.

"You did exactly what I expected. I know you, Anderson. I am aware that there was no room for a fourth passenger in that plane. That's the only reason that I didn't insist on coming with you. I was worried to death about you."

She was clearly proud and exasperated about what I had done, but she had been worried sick. I squeezed her hand.

"Now what should I do with you knowing the scare you put into me? Just think about that while I kiss you. Again. And again."

I began to see what she meant, and I was about to rise to the occasion when she stood up, grabbed my hand and led me down to the sea. We tore off our shoes and walked into the surf in our bare feet as the cold, salty water climbed out of the vast Pacific and curled around our calves and then retreated, pulling suds and seaweed around our ankles as we kissed in the moonlight.

Rachel Tackles a Mastermind

Rachel awakened the morning after our incursion into Mexico in a buoyant mood. She was all smiles, and she made me feel as if I was going to have one of the greatest days of my life. We breakfasted on piping hot coffee and waffles with whipped butter and Vermont maple syrup. Rachel had cleared a place for our settings among all our computers, notes, and paper diagrams. Having let me brood for a while silently over all that we had to do today, she spoke.

"I had a good time last night. I just wanted to thank you for, well, everything."

I was both flattered and alarmed. I chose my words carefully, asking after a moment's pause, "Have you decided to move on?"

She came over to me and kissed me on the mouth ruffling my hair. A concerned look crossed her face, and she sat down with finality as if to say that she was not going anywhere at all.

I smiled at her ruefully. "Things are likely to get rough ahead. In the next stages of our operation, we're nearing a climax of sorts." Rachel appeared both alarmed and intrigued.

"Will the Agency help with some of what we have left to do? For example, searches of the ports for weapons of mass destruction materials would best be handled by sensors and roving teams with dogs."

I was very proud of her for thinking about the operational implications without my prodding. "That's right, Rachel. That work has already begun in earnest. My team is feeding the various search teams data from our analyses of cargo traffic to those ports. The terrorists had managed to make a mockery of our expensive systems of sensors that were supposed to keep weapons of mass destruction out of the country. The contractors who were paid billions of dollars will have to cover their asses with claims of misuse by port authorities. The government will be upset enough to spend more billions on the same nonsense hardware and software. Congress will be outraged in public and clueless in private. With all the commotion blocking any forward motion, we'll have to jump to other questions that we could find the answers for, without officialdom."

Rachel listened quietly to my tirade, stroking my hand as if to let me know she understood and to calm me.

When my harridan boss, the Deputy Director of Operations, learned of the in-and-out shootings in Mexico, she, fortunately, made no connection between the Blomfelds and me. The tail number on the airplane that we used had been painted over to lead anyone who saw it to a blind canyon, but no one saw the plane coming or going. If it had been a crime, it would have been the perfect crime.

I circulated my picture of the leader of the Iranian terrorists within the Agency to get an ID. The deceased was a terrorist leader known to be active in South America. I also circulated my picture of David Hartnet, and to my surprise the man was identified as a terrorist of American birth having any of five aliases on four continents. I knew that the Iranian terrorist leader would be replaced by another Quds Force operative directed by the General of the Quds Force himself. That led me nowhere productive. I also knew that the man called Vibius was not the mastermind of the operation. He was just the demented but gay leader of other disaffected gays in San Diego. I dared not send Ruth's brother Ryan into Vibius's territory again. If a contract had been put out for someone of Ryan's description, I would not have been surprised.

During the out brief at the hamburger joint, I had asked the Blomfelds to assure that the Mossad would follow up on the international scene and try to find the mastermind behind what was happening in the U.S. I did not think much would come of the request, but then I did not factor the gratitude of the Israelis for my having engineered the extraction of a Mossad agent from Mexico. Ruth told me that the Institute was more than grateful. They felt indebted to me because I had saved her brother's life. Still, I figured that the best people to find who was the puppet master behind the scenes was my team and me—and, of course, Rachel.

"Rachel, many ladies of discernment will read Good Housekeeping or Elle at the breakfast table while their husbands pore over Investor's Business Daily, or the New York Times. That is decidedly not our style. Here you sit surfing the net looking for underground dealers in weapons of mass destruction of all varieties. Please pass the marmalade."

Absentmindedly, Rachel passed the marmalade. "Want some more coffee? I think the answer to our question might lie in plain view and be available from open-source literature."

"I just refreshed us on the coffee. You were distracted. Agencies try to keep the big dealers under control by shining a light on their activities as a warning to them and their customers. The world of black arms deals is minuscule, and everyone in the trade knows everyone else in it. They all know the big deals that are being done, and they place their bids on the work just like ordinary suppliers."

"I think that two men fit the bill as our prime suspects. One's a fat Turkish billionaire named Emil Bogadsu, and the other's a handsome and dashing upstart, a German named Hans Schroeder who cut his teeth working for the USSR's KGB and now works for the Russian Federation State Security. Of the two I think Schroeder is more likely to be our man. He is currently in South Africa working with the infamous weapons of mass destruction salesman Wouter Basson. Schroeder is due to return to his Liechtenstein mansion in one week. All of this information is from open sources that anyone can read."

Since Rachel's new target was reputed to be a gambler and a womanizer, Rachel asked, "What do women of fashion wear at the more expensive casinos in the Duchy of Liechtenstein?" She saw my look of bewilderment and countermanded herself. Her fingers flew over advanced search routines that brought the EU fashion world into high relief. She stopped suddenly to ask, "What's your budget for my trip to Liechtenstein?"

"It'll be whatever you require."

"Then I'll need a minimum of fifty-thousand dollars, not including my fee, which will be another fifty-thousand dollars for two weeks' work. For security, you should consider sending Ruth Blomfeld with me for another hundred grand. Of course, the Mossad might fund Ruth's travel to save the CIA some money."

"Maybe we should let the Blomfelds know the plan?"

"I'll let them know we'll be returning to the hamburger joint for discussions," Rachel called Ruth to arrange the meeting. Ryan was busy so he would not be able to come.

At the meeting, Ruth and Rachel did most of the talking, and it was clear to me that they were very excited at the prospect of bagging Hans Schroeder. Ruth asked me point blank whether assassination might be sanctioned. I told her that it would probably not be authorized without hard evidence of his complicity.

"The Director of the CIA will have to request a Presidential Finding to get the go-ahead for a kill."

Ruth shook her head in mock sympathy as if to say, "Poor you." Mossad evidently did not have our American scruples about assassinations, though I knew that they had a similar need for top-level approval for a hit. Ruth thought that she and Rachel should share the bridal suite at the most expensive hotel in the Duchy. Using that as their command center, they would do their planning and, possibly, lure their prey to his undoing. I had organized liaisons like this before, and I was concerned about a possible shift of venue in the middle of the mission. I, therefore, suggested that Ryan and I book a suite in a nearby hotel as security.

With a single voice the women objected. Ruth was the more vocal of the two.

"The fastest way to scare Hans Schroeder is to give his bodyguards reason for suspicion. We two women should go alone into the lion's den and get the lion. I know how to use sodium pentothal and do implemented interrogation. I've been successful extracting intelligence from Hamas and Hezbollah agents. This German won't be a problem."

That sealed the plan. The women would fly to London for a two-day shopping spree and makeover. Then they would fly to Liechtenstein with everything they needed for their job. Ryan and I would continue using our separate command centers and monitor events from the U.S.

Ruth seemed like the child in the candy store when she and Rachel boarded their plane in LA. Here she was traveling with a woman for whom she had more than the usual respect. Rachel was looking her best because I trusted her to do a solo mission with Ruth as her backup and technical support.

The air transport and transfers went perfectly. After they had arrived at their destination, I received daily reports of their progress. Ryan and I fed the women agents data about the whereabouts of Hans Schroeder and the general situation on the ground in London and the Duchy.

Ruth and Rachel took a suite at the Renaissance Inn in Kensington and spent two days shopping and getting their hair and nails done in the high fashion district of Mayfair. When they flew to Liechtenstein, they looked like minor royalty on a fling. Their jewelry alone would have attracted every gold digger and wastrel in Europe.

Using Mossad intelligence assets without divulging his purpose, Ryan discovered the name of Hans Schroeder's favorite casino, and he relayed information about Schroeder's nocturnal habits to Ruth. As Rachel had estimated, the cover charge for entering Schroeder's favorite casino was ten thousand Euros. Rachel thought that they should plan to do everything that they had intended to do in a single night. Hans Schroeder was fast, and he liked fast women. Rachel figured that he would be no problem.

The entire operation worked better than I had anticipated. The women, posing as distant cousins and countesses, made Hans Schroeder's acquaintance at the bar of the casino. After he had bought them their third drink each, he asked where they were staying and whether they had ever entertained a single gentleman together. Rachel and Ruth looked scandalized at first. After their initial shock faded away, they glanced at one another shyly before batting their eyes at their target. Hans Schroeder got their message loud and clear. He dismissed his bodyguards, saying that he would return to his mansion in the morning and escorted the two women to his Bentley for the drive to their hotel.

Rachel gave me the play-by-play in the bridal suite. It was a classic case of seduction. Hans could not decide which woman to make love to first, so the ladies stripped and danced in front of him while he drank to clear his mind. By the time they had made him admit that he could not choose between them, they maneuvered the man to the enormous bridal bed and stripped him naked on it. They then took turns with Hans Schroeder with malicious glee to prove to him that some women were literally insatiable. He tried to hold up his manhood through a sixth erection, but he failed. He did not even feel the needle in his arm that fed him sodium pentothal.

Rachel recorded the entire interrogation, and the details of Hans Schroeder's deals for weapons of mass destruction were extensive, even encyclopedic. Under the effects of the truth serum and the charms of his two ladies, Hans Schroeder bragged about his commercial conquests. He also told them about his contacts and the governments with which he regularly dealt. Boasting that he was a major supplier to Iran for nuclear and centrifuge technologies, he had assisted clients who wanted the weapons of mass destruction in Iraq and Syria, including the General of the Quds Force. Not just anyone could arrange for the transshipments so that embargoes could be avoided. When Ruth pressed him, he told them the bank accounts he used with their account numbers and approximate current holdings. The weapons of mass destruction in the pipeline tripped off his tongue, along with the protocols of payments for materials that had reached their destinations. Yes, he knew about shipments to Philadelphia and Chicago because he had arranged them. He had arranged similar shipments for Hamas. Their materials were right now underground in Palestine waiting to be used against the Jews. He said this with a smile of great satisfaction.

The expression on Ruth's face when she heard about the weapons of mass destruction for Hamas was eloquent. Rachel knew then that Hans Schroeder might not live until the morning. In fact, however, Ruth was pragmatic. She was not a bloodthirsty killer but showed panache and wit. She decided to love the man to death. For that, she broke open a pack of Cialis tabs and had him wash them down with vodka. She continued interrogating him until his speech slurred beyond recognition and his member became an obdurate battering ram. Ruth used lubricants to assure safe passage, and then mounted the helpless German and gave him the ride of his life.

With a mix of horror and amusement, Rachel said that Hans Schroeder's erection lasted for fully six hours, from midnight until dawn. Ruth rode him, applying lubricants as necessary to keep her from being harmed inside. Rachel spelled her for a while, but Ruth saw to it that the final stretch was hers alone. When Hans Schroeder finally expired, he had the most seraphic look on his face that Rachel had ever seen on a man, me included. Ruth herself looked mightily oversexed, but happy that she had caused this German pig to die in her arms after giving her the dildo job of a lifetime. With a determined, cold and disgusted voice, she said that she would not remember Hans, but she would remember what he sold to Hamas.

The women took long, separate showers, each taking the time to communicate their reports to Ryan and me with attached voice recordings. Ruth requested that Ryan forward the recording immediately to Mossad for action. Rachel texted me that Hans had died of natural causes in Ruth's loving arms. I laughed for fifteen minutes at the idea of that and then texted, "LMAO" to Rachel, together with my recommendation that the two women immediately vacate the hotel and the Duchy. I advised them to pay all their bills with large tips and to tell the Maitre d' that their businessman friend had passed out from strenuous exertions during the night and that he would very much appreciate not being disturbed until their normal 1 p.m. check out time.

Ruth and Rachel's exit from the Duchy was flawless. They went over the border on the train to France looking like graduate students with backpacks, braids, and wire-framed granny glasses. As they rode, they played video games and snubbed the male students who wanted to ingratiate themselves. A lesbian pair, the male students thought, man-eaters, all. When Ruth overheard their bitter chatter, she smiled maliciously, put her arm around Rachel and kissed her on the mouth long and hard. It was something she had wanted to do for weeks, and having the chance was too hard for her to resist.

Rachel told me later that Ruth had the sweetest breath she had ever experienced in another person. She said it was the panther's breath of European mythology often associated with Jesus Christ. I thought, "Oh, Christ!" until she burst out into laughter and tickled me mercilessly. She confessed that the worst part of her mission had been her turn to ride the wild Hans in the night. The exchanges had been executed to perfection, without a break in the action. First Ruth was off and Rachel was on and away; then Rachel was off and Ruth was riding for the finish line. Very sincerely Rachel said that for the first time in her life she knew the pros and cons of the best dildos. The pro was that the ride need never end. The con was that the ride might never end.

"Mechanical sex has always repulsed me. What do you think?" This was a subject we had never broached, and she sincerely wanted to know what I thought.

"I don't care what you think about the mechanics: I only—" Rachel screwed up her face. "Don't ever take the blue pill. I can manage all the chemistry you'll need all by myself. Your sensitivity and charm plus my patience and skill are worth all the dildos in creation. As for sex with women, after Ruth I have a new appreciation for what that means. I want to be sure that you actually do find me as delightful as I think you must. Ruth's kissing me was a rude awakening that I'd rather not encounter again. I'm an inveterate heterosexual and proud of it." Rachel's disgust when she spoke of Ruth's kiss was palpable. I was delighted to have proof of my partner's heterosexuality and flattered by her thoughts about us.

"I like you that way, but I have no opinion of lesbians because I've never knowingly kissed one. Perhaps I should kiss Ruth to see about her panther's breath?"

Rachel pummeled me lightly with her fists and raised her head for a kiss, which I gave her gladly. She melted in my arms and placed her tiny hands against my chest. I put my arms around her and hugged her gently. She trembled.

"Just keep holding me, Anderson, and never let me go."

Rachel and I had a lot to say to each other, but we needed no words to say what we felt. We used the language of our hands and our mouths and every other part of our bodies. What precisely did we say to each other? I cannot put it into words. My raven-haired lover gave herself to me with the same candor in the same sense of wonder and delight as I gave myself to her. We held each other's gazes and embraced each other for much longer than usual. We felt each other's presence in everything we did, whether we were together or separated. We did not take because everything was freely given and shared in such a way that my being male and her being female were part of some larger coalescence in which we were conjoined.

We did not even try to break Hans Schroeder's record performance, which will not be chronicled in any of the record books. What would that prove? I once saw on the Internet a picture of a strong man naked with his two legs straining on two boulders wide apart. The man's penis was distended and enormous. The man's gargantuan penis was bound with a rope, and to the other end of the rope was tied an enormous stone that hung pendulous and stretched almost but not quite to the ground between the boulders. It strained my imagination to think that a penis could withstand the strain of the weight and strangulation without breaking off. Yet the picture showed that it could and did withstand it in this one instance. Why would a man want to prove his manhood with such grotesque demonstration? I do not know.

As for Hans Schroeder, the arms merchant, he did not choose to use so much Cialis that he could stand being screwed by two women for six hours until he died. He did, however, elect to sell weapons of mass destruction repeatedly to the worst terrorists in the world. Was it justice that brought him to his end—or pleasure? I like to think it was both. What went through Ruth's mind while she administered her rough justice, I cannot say. When I asked Rachel about this, she said that the look in Ruth's eyes as she rode that symbol of Aryan oppression was wild and triumphant. It was as if she were trying to empty the evil out of the man with her vagina, pulling upwards with equal force to the downward force of that crude pendulous stone suspended from that rope in the picture. The erection had not broken even when the man had died. Such was the cost and price of manhood. Such was the triumph of eternal womanhood. In her showering afterward, Ruth had scrubbed herself inside and out to rid her body of any sign of Hans Schroeder.

"Ruth was pleased with what she had done. She said that she would do it again to such trash as Hans Schroeder. I've never heard a voice that held such cold hatred as hers. She had literally loved to kill him." Rachel had been both amazed and terrified by Ruth's ruthless performance.

I watched the news broadcasts for the announcement of Hans Schroeder's death, but none hit the major stations in Europe or the US. For some time afterward I wondered whether the man had survived the ordeal administered by Ruth. Finally as I read through accounts of arms trades gone awry and an increased tempo of competition in the underworld of arms, all the signs of Hans Schroeder's death fell into place. The man was surely dead. Other arms merchants would fill the void that his death had caused. His bodyguards would have found other employers as bad as or perhaps even worse than he.

I did not sanitize the recordings of Hans Schroeder spilling his life's secrets into the lap of the Mossad agent Ruth Blomfeld. I sent them raw and unedited to several CIA operatives who were in the arms interdiction business. They wondered where I could have possibly gotten such a treasure trove of intelligence. I told them that sources and methods would be violated if I told them where I got the recording. They understood the rules. They did not have the visuals that would have given away the interrogation secrets. I had only sent the oral tapes, not the visuals, which I destroyed. What the Blomfelds and Mossad did with their copies, I did not know and I did not care to know. The results of their having the records meant that we could assuredly take down all those transactions that Hans Schroeder had compromised. Those included the weapons of mass destruction at our U.S. ports.

Of course, the harridan Deputy Director for Operations was shrieking at me and threatening me on her cell phone every day for a full week because of the unorthodox tactics that I used, always going around the system, never telling her what I was going to do beforehand. At times, I thought that I should send Ruth to her to see what she could do to change the tyro's attitude. I decided that I would not inflict that torture on Ruth, my comrade in arms and protector of Rachel. Besides, Ruth and I had in common our infatuation with Rachel the raven-haired. We understood each other through that common bond.

"Ruth, could you have done the job on Hans Schroeder without Rachel's assistance?" Ruth gave me an odd, sidelong look before she said, "Perhaps, but I might have hurt myself without a relief at the critical moment. Hans Schroeder never would have told his bodyguards to take the night off if he had not been so smitten with Rachel. She provided the tipping point that won the day for the operation. She also gave me the energy to demonstrate to her what she could do to a man who offended her." She gave me an oddly admonitory stare. She did not frighten me, but I could see how she might frighten others.

"You definitely made an indelible impression on her." I recalled Rachel trembling against my chest with her hands pressed firmly against me.

"I was proud to have used my sex to destroy an enemy of Israel. Guns, garrotes, and knives are so very mechanical, after all. Of course, strangling the man with my bare hands would have been even more satisfying than sexing him to death. But I confess that I didn't have the strength to have strangled Hans Schroeder as he so richly deserved." Ruth delivered this diatribe in a seething rage. Her admission that she did not have the strength to strangle her prey surprised me with its candor.

"Your brother Ryan might have done that, don't you think?"

"He never could have gotten past the man's security guards like we two women did. Besides, using my vagina sent the message that I preferred to send. It was his conduit to hell." When she told me that, I had no doubt about her warning. Hers was the conduit by which she would send all males to hell if she had the chance. I shuddered to think about her in that way. Ruth knew what she was saying, and she knew I understood her in a very personal way. She also knew what Rachel felt about me, and while she hated to consider it, she knew that I was the best thing for Rachel at this time in her life. Ruth would permit our love, but in protest. I did not care what Ruth thought as long as everything sat well with Rachel.

I asked Rachel what she thought of doing missions in Europe like the one that she had just done.

"I did not mind the mission. Ruth was great company. Hans Schroeder was a lecher and a creep. His bodyguards were scary goons, and we were lucky they stood back and let Hans Schroeder accompany Ruth and me alone. I'm sad for Ruth who can never find what she wants, which is to be a man in woman's form. A sex change would be too simple a solution and all wrong. Ruth had on many occasions made a move on me, but finally she understood that I'm not a lesbian and never will be one. Even if I'd been so inclined, Ruth would not have been satisfied with me because there would be no way for a woman to do to her what she wanted done to herself. Ruth is complex. I also am complex and somewhat conflicted."

"What do you mean when you say you're conflicted?"

Rachel thought deeply before she answered my question. She looked inwards and I thought she might cry.

"I have strong feelings for you, and Ruth knew that I also have very strong feelings for her. She said that she knew how much I valued her having freedom but that she also knew how much I was concerned that she was safe. She told me she wanted to be whatever pleased me. She knew that I wanted to please her infinitely more than I wanted to be pleased. So there she was caught between our best ideals and our deepest fears."

"Deepest fears?"

"I feared losing you when you were in Mexico. You feared losing me when I barely escaped from a beach house filled with explosives."

"I feared for your life during the entire European adventure."

Rachel smiled and shook her head. She came to me and kissed me, and then she laid her head on my shoulder and wept, sobbing deeply and weeping so that my cheek was wet with her tears.

We shared wine that evening on the back porch overlooking the swelling ocean. By starlight the vast deep seemed not to fall away but to rise from the shore and arch up into the heavens. Rachel had my hand in hers, and she drew it to her cheek and then kissed it.

"I cannot believe our luck," she said with a tremulous voice filled with emotion. "I am the happiest woman alive with you. You make me whole. I do not know what I would do without you."

My heart was ready to leap right out of my chest. I wanted to hug her tight and tell her what she meant to me. I honestly did not know what I would do without her. At this impasse, instead of launching into the great unknowns of my feelings, I tried to steer our mood back to something manageable by asking her whether she wanted me to count out her money now or later. She turned to me and held me at arm's length.

"Sir, let us retire, you and I, and if you want to count something, let's try orgasms or shouts of ecstasy and joy. Tomorrow is soon enough to think of money. Tonight I do not want to think or count at all, but you can count and when you have done with me, you shall not have done at all."

As always, Rachel was right on the mark. We soared through the night like eagles mating in the high air without a safety net, wings beating together as they fall thousands of feet in ecstasy, only breaking when they almost reach the earth. And then they soar again together as eagles do always.

Rachel on a Roll

In retrospect, I should have seen it coming. Someone as beautiful and talented as Rachel was a natural recruit as a stringer for the Mossad. Rachel had been tested on her mission to Liechtenstein in the company of Ruth Blomfeld. In checking out Rachel's background while she was essentially a hostage at the house on Mulholland Drive, Mossad Headquarters in Jerusalem would have realized that as a person with an entirely clean record, free of all Agency connections, Rachel was a rare commodity in the global espionage game. I had seen the value of that, and it's why I recruited her. Now Ruth Blomfeld, with or without Mossad Headquarters sanction, was trying to co-opt Rachel to do Mossad business on the same or better terms than what she did for me. The thing was, her first assignment for the Institute was sanctioned by me because I thought it a natural extension of our weapons of mass destruction mission.

After our night of hot, passionate lovemaking celebrating Rachel's successful mission in Liechtenstein and return to the safe house on the beach, I received the call for help from Ryan Blomfeld. Mossad had traced the purchase of the weapons of mass destruction for Hamas to a self-exiled Saudi Prince, Ibn Abud bin Sultan, aka 'the Prince', playboy and billionaire who now resided in Mayfair, right in the heart of London. The man was an outrageous lecher who once boasted that he had enjoyed the charms of more fashion models than Vogue, Elle and Mademoiselle had ever featured all together. The Prince's first wife ran his harem with an iron rolling pin, but she could not control her husband's extracurricular activities. She probably knew about the separate posh quarters where the Prince entertained his concubines, but what could she do about it? She had her jewelry and her income to protect, and the Prince had a fiery temper when angered. The Prince's appetites gravitated to black-haired women, and he hated pretenders so much that he personally examined each of his lovers to be sure their hair had natural color. In one case, he had DNA samples analyzed just to be sure. In another case, the Prince discovered that one of his black haired models was really a German blonde. The unfortunate woman was found drugged, nude and cleanly shaven in one of the seedier East End hotels. When the tabloids got the story, the model's career ended. She was last seen at a low-end brothel near the train terminal in Amsterdam.

At our usual table in the back of the hamburger joint, the Blomfelds, Rachel and I met to discuss the situation and the Blomfelds' plan of attack. Ruth said that they could not kill the Prince because that would put Israel in an even more awkward position vis-à-vis Saudi Arabia than usual. If, however, the Prince were to become a victim of his own gallivanting lifestyle, his family might be embarrassed so much that his allowance would be substantially reduced. That would at minimum curtail his ability to finance the terrorists who were bent on destroying the Jewish State. Ryan added with a particularly nasty sneer that if some connection of the Prince to the London gay community could be arranged without attribution to Mossad, the Prince would be finished as a global player. The upshot of the

Blomfelds' thinking was that Rachel was the perfect lure for the Prince. They had been given clandestine funding by Mossad for the in-and-out operation. They believed that the Prince's fall would send a message to other financiers of global terror. The United States, they said, would be a little closer to safety as a result. At that point, I probably should have thrown the bullshit flag, but Rachel said that she was game for the mission. I nodded, and Rachel was seconded to the Blomfelds until the mission had ended. I said that my only condition was that the Blomfelds guarantee Rachel's security and safe passage to London and back to LA. They agreed, and Rachel went back to Mulholland Drive with the Blomfelds to prepare for her mission.

Generally, you don't associate comedy with Mossad operations. I can think of a few howlers—like the Israeli co-ed hit team that got caught in traffic during the New Zealand earthquake—but, on the whole, the Mossad was quiet, deadly and efficient. For the Prince, the Blomfelds created one for the record books, and Rachel was at stage center right up under the limelight.

My information was limited due to the Blomfelds' silence, but from what I gathered, Rachel arrived in London as planned in company with the Blomfelds under different names, and all stayed at various hotels in Kensington. Rachel, dressed in her zillion-shekel finery, had no trouble catching the roving eyes of the Prince. She was on her way with the Prince in his Rolls Royce to his secret hideaway when suddenly two black cars blocked the Prince's Rolls front and rear on a back street. Hooded figures coshed the Prince's driver before he could react, and the Prince and his consort for the evening were abducted with black bags over their heads. Rachel said that she played no part in the subsequent drama, but Ruth had drugged and given the

Prince a full-body shave to prepare him for his triumphant entry into paradise. She had done this wearing nothing but a mask and flaunting her blonde hair before his eyes as she wielded her straightedge razor.

When the Prince had been properly prepared, Ryan entered naked in his mask with two naked, old friends from the East End gay community. The two burly gay men escorted the groggy Prince to an all-night gay pride indoor parade where the Prince, naked as the day he was born and stupefied by the drugs that Ruth had administered, was installed on his triumphal throne, which was composed of naked participants and surrounded by a debauch of equally naked LGBT revelers. The paparazzi photo op commenced just as the Prince raised his cornucopia and the crowd surrounding him began to cheer, repeatedly calling for the Prince to speak. Before long the London police arrived to escort the revelers to the safety of jail. Satisfied that the entire proceedings had been filmed in quality HDTV format, Ryan sent the uncut footage, together with a brief video life story of the Prince and footage of actual beheadings of homosexuals in Riyadh, to every media outlet from Singapore to the Channel Islands.

The astonished media could not believe their luck, and they rushed to publish everything before the Saudi royal family could initiate damage control. And what could the royal family say anyway? That the scion of the King of the Kingdom of Saudi Arabia was not a rake-hellion? That the Prince was not associated with late-night sexual adventures outside the sanctity of his harem? That the Prince abstained from using drugs? Who would believe the story that the Prince had been abducted?

Predictably, the Prince's chauffeur wrote a deposition that the Prince had been abducted, but he could not describe the abductors or anything particular about how the abduction had happened. He was recalled to the Kingdom and later was beheaded for abandoning the Prince in his hour of need. The Prince's allowance was summarily cut off and his bank accounts frozen. In the blizzard of scandals, the Prince could not give a good description of the lady who had accompanied him out off the casino. Security cameras did contain some footage of Rachel, but no one could say who she was. A woman answering her description had checked out of a hotel in Kensington and vanished from London without a trace.

The yellow press did not care what the Kingdom officials said or did. They knew exactly what kinds of headlines sold copy. "Gay Saudi Prince Outed in East End Orgy" and "Bugger Your Neighbor Wahhabis?" and "Good Night, Sweet Prince!" were my favorites. Even Al Jazeera got into the act and published all the copies they could muster. Sharp words were exchanged backstage between Saudi Arabia and Qatar before Al Jazeera expunged the footage, but it was far too late to put the scandal back in Pandora's Box. A thousand YouTube renditions crowded the Net. Twitter, FaceBook, and LinkedIn were alive with speculations and conspiracy theories, many of them stimulated by a special Mossad team in Jerusalem. They took the occasion to out every closet gay in the Middle East who was not Israeli. The LGBT community worldwide played the "Gay Prince" footage for months on a continuous loop in every gay bar in the world. A major producer invested in a Broadway play about the outing of the Prince, but he was bribed not to proceed by the Saudi royal family. CNN tried to land a contract for exclusive rights to interview and exploit the Prince, who was now reduced to beggary if not buggery, to make a living because he no longer had an unlimited account funded by Saudi Aramco's oil and gas proceeds. As a result, the Saudi royal family agreed to pay the Prince and CNN one-million a month for two years to keep the lid on the story.

Rachel's cameo appearance set off a frenzied media search for the "goddess" model that had lured the Saudi Prince into his terminal den of vice and iniquity. Her moving image was an Internet sensation for about four weeks until word went out that she had been an unfortunate victim of that fateful night. Coincidentally, a badly mutilated dead body had been discovered caught in the London sewage system. The body's head had been cut off and never found. The corpse proved that the decedent was actually a blonde who had dyed her hair raven black for some reason. DNA analysis indicated that the murdered woman had been Palestinian. All further inquiry into the woman's death met a dead end.

Rachel and I were relieved that the media had finally been diverted. We wondered for a while how the story about the murdered Palestinian woman had been manufactured. When I asked Ruth, she told me with annoyance not to look too deeply into that because it was a Mossad matter. I was disturbed by Ruth's veiled revelation, but I said nothing to her at the time. I did not tell Rachel about that critical information. She did not have the need to know, and the knowledge might have hurt her.

At our hamburger joint celebration, the Blomfelds waxed eloquent about Rachel's stunning performance in London. She had been the lynchpin for the operation, and she never had to succumb to the Prince's embraces. Mossad had learned that the Prince had been treated after the gay indoor parade for sexually transmitted diseases with powerful drugs. The physician, who was a Mossad agent, told Ryan it was lucky that the Prince's intended concubine had not slept with him. Rachel shuddered to think about that. She said that she found him repugnant, repellant and unclean. The Blomfelds nodded as if to say, "What else would you expect?"

"Do you Blomfelds have any other ideas for which Rachel might prove useful to your agency?" I needed to know whether she was going to be tasked again soon or not. I did not mind her doing another Mossad mission, but we had other fish to fry. I wanted to know whether I could count on Rachel's availability for my operation.

Ruth answered, "Not for now, Anderson, but we will be looking for new opportunities. She did an excellent job!"

So Rachel and I returned to the beach safe house, and I tried to catch up on operational developments over the last five weeks.

It was good, from my point of view, for Rachel and me to settle into a routine again. Rachel needed to wind down slowly, and so she spent a lot of time walking on the beach and reading. I began making checklists and sifting through the myriad of data about transshipments that ultimately led to weapons of mass destruction in U.S. ports. My team had been busy tying up loose ends. They had averaged a coup every two weeks with weapons of mass destruction caches found by our Agency port teams in Chicago—where the biological weapons were found—and Philadelphia—where the chemical weapons were found. The big picture was clarifying in a horrific manner. The scope and dimensions of the plot were staggeringly large. If every weapons of mass destruction cache had been orchestrated perfectly, the U.S. government would have been rendered defunct in the face of unprecedented mass casualties and sheer terror. Because all World War II-era safeguards and processes had been eliminated, the only recourse for the U.S. government in the face of such an attack would have been nationwide Marshall Law. The nation would have become a military dictatorship, all standard patterns would have been disrupted, and life as we know it would have been changed utterly. The prospect made me sick to my stomach, and I got the urge from time to time to take revenge on those who would perpetrate such mayhem anywhere.

My team began to make connections with disconcerting results. They began to understand how the weapons of mass destruction had gotten from their inland locations to the ports where they had been containerized and shipped to the U.S. In some cases, the Iranian Quds Force or the Syrians had been responsible for overland transport. In other instances, the Russian Federation had clearly been responsible. Signature analysis indicated that all found radionuclide materials had ultimately come from Iran or Russia. Labeling and signature analysis indicated that all found biological and chemical weapons originated in Iraq, Syria, Iran or Russia. I reviewed the bidding on transport overseas to verify that all transshipments had been first carried in Quds Force container ships and then carried in container vessels owned or chartered by either the People's Republic of China or the Democratic People's Republic of Korea. At the time, I felt both frustrated and discouraged. The terrorists were still way out in front of the collective efforts we had managed to marshal against them. So what had we accomplished so far? With our operations, we had managed to take out a financier and a middleman in arms trafficking and a low-level operator behind the attacks on the American homeland. The authorities had not yet identified and apprehended the terrorist cells that were supposed to execute the plan. For all that, my team and I had not yet identified the originator and architect of the plan itself. The situation was unsatisfactory because on any day of their choosing the terrorists could paralyze and shut down the American economy.

When I thought that Rachel had recovered from her London mission, I laid out all our evidence and used her as a sounding board for my latest thoughts. She was an excellent listener, always nodding at the right moments and responding in the right ways. She was able to pick out threads that I could not see because I was so close to the data. She listened carefully to my data and analysis, and then she thought for a moment and exclaimed, "Russia!" I asked her to elaborate.

"Where during the Cold War did all these countries get their knowledge of weapons of mass destruction? It was certainly not from the U.S. You don't make weapons of mass destruction without a lot of technical knowledge and expertise—generations of experts."

"I agree wholeheartedly. So where does this line of reasoning lead us?"

Rachel thought for a moment, and then she pressed right on.

"Essentially, any nuclear, biological or chemical weapon can be traced to its origins in a major power. So weren't all those biological and chemical weapons you mentioned first made in the USSR and then exported to or cloned in Iraq, Iran, Syria or North Korea?"

"Yes, that is the case." So far, her reasoning was according to current Agency thinking.

"We in the West figured that since the USSR was gone, its legacy was also gone. This was not true. Didn't you tell me that the genesis of suicide bombing was in Russia, not the Middle East?"

"Yes, and it was." I had traced the lines of influence down to the Russian agents who were responsible for both the strategy and execution of it.

"So why couldn't a big plan for attacking America originate in Russia?" This was among the unspoken ideas harbored in the deepest shadows at the Agency. It was the great dragon that threatened analysts' with sleepless nights and endless labyrinths of frantic research by day.

"I catch your drift now. Go on, Rachel, I'm listening. You have my full attention."

"Only our propaganda stopped us from following leads that traced from September 11, 2001, back to support and planning from Russia and China."

"I have to admit that we put the blinders on for many reasons. It was wrong to do so, but those of us who knew it was wrong were overridden." I did not want to interrupt her flow of thoughts by giving her the details of the cover-up.

"You said that in matters of state, some things are too large to investigate."

"Yes, I did. And they often are beyond the scope and reach of federal agencies, even the CIA."

"You always preached that policy gets in the way. You said that sometimes you have to discover ways to circumvent policy to achieve justice."

"Always."

"I believed you then. Did you mean it?"

Then she smiled and shrugged, rose from the divan and bounced into the kitchen to make us some coffee.

I sat brooding until she brought me a piping hot cup of coffee.

"I believed what I had told you earlier about policy. I still believe it."

I now had to stop to think things through because she had put the ball squarely back in my court. I took her points, and now I had to feed them back in a manner that could give us a way forward.

I sighed and said, "Okay, just for argument, let's consider that Russia or some legacy Communist faction in Russia wanted to crush the wellspring of capitalism and global prosperity. Let's further posit that 911 was such a plot but it failed because of its limited scope. After all, the World Trade Center attack was only part of that picture, which also included a biological weapon in the form of anthrax. Still, the scope of that attack was relatively contained when compared with the plot we have uncovered. Who in what setting did the planning? Who put together all the pieces? Who had the personnel, the funding and the perseverance to do all of this?"

"Now you are framing the questions like Anderson and not like some Agency lackey looking for promotion by connecting only a few dots." Rachel playfully nudged me while she nodded and smiled. "I can't give you the answers, but now you are asking the right questions, I think."

I drifted into deep thought about the situation, with Rachel watching me expectantly. I must have brooded for fifteen minutes without either of us speaking a word. Then she sprang up and announced that she was going to fix dinner.

"What do you want for dinner? I'm planning creamed asparagus soup, filet mignon and raspberry sherbet for dessert. Okay?"

I must have nodded.

"Okay. I'll get right to it. Start getting me some answers, please, because I am already hungry and not a little randy too."

While Rachel was puttering in the kitchen, I did a large freehand drawing on brown butcher paper. At the top I wrote "Boris" for the USSR and Russia and from that I drew lines to represent the directions of USSR/Russian influence. I then had to write "Mao" for China in block letters, and I drew lines to represent the directions of PRC/Chinese influence. I wrote "Middle East," and I drew lines to represent the directions of Iranian and Saudi influence. This influence was particularly interesting because of what we learned from our contact with the enemy in Mexico.

By the time dinner was ready, I had come to realize that the key to our mystery was labeled BORIS. All other influences were tributaries feeding the single great power that we once feared as the USSR and now we were beginning to fear again as Russia.

Rachel said, "You must be on the right track now, though you're sounding like a conspiracy theorist." This made me so rip-snorting mad that I sprang from my chair and began pacing the room.

I finally exploded into a tirade and waved my hands in the air as I spoke in anger. "The best way to defeat a strategic argument is to label it as a conspiracy theory. Do you know how many thousands of documented cases of assassinations there are of investigative journalists who had come too close to the truth while exploring the viability of so-called conspiracy theories? I've known excellent agents of the CIA who were ostracized and forced out of the Agency, not because they were wrong in their analysis but because they were right."

Rachel was listening to me, but she bustled around bringing dinner to the table. Our feast was set by the time I had finished venting.

"I believe you. Let's eat!" Rachel had not informed me that our cream of asparagus soup would be served cold, but it was excellent as was everything else she ever prepared for us. The filet mignon had been brushed lightly over the fire just as I liked it. She had opened a bottle of Cabernet Sauvignon and let it breathe. It was excellent with the beef. The raspberry sherbet was served for dessert with a wedge of lime and a spring of mint leaf.

"Coffee and Lindt chocolate topped off the feast," I said with a broad smile.

She frowned and corrected me harshly. Waving her finger side to side, she rose from her chair and took me by the hand.

"That's no topping off. I'll show you how we shall top off the feast, in bed. I have already turned down the covers and laid out the towels in the bathroom. So turn off the lights and come with me now. You have been working much too hard for too long. It is Nirvana time, and I am ready for you to take me there."

Rachel's History Lesson

Rachel was having second thoughts about the persons behind the planning for the terrorist action against the U.S. The Al Qaeda leader, Osama bin Laden was dead, but his vision had not been expansive enough to encompass a plot that involved simultaneous weapons of mass destruction attacks on a half dozen of the largest U.S. ports, including New York-New Jersey, LA-Long Beach and Chicago. Yes, the scope of the attack seemed geopolitically to be on a level with the old USSR, and many of the old war horses of the USSR were still in power in Russia. Still, she was bothered by the thought that the plan was the brainchild of the current regime. She also had doubts that the current regime had the guts and determination to execute such a plan, even through cutouts, when its failure meant exposure.

I had to interject a thought at this point. The main outline of the plan would mean nothing significant if many pieces of the plan were to be interdicted before execution. Already the plan had been exposed by the Agency's activities, and the government was bolstering its surveillance, defense, and infrastructure to deal with the aftermath of a weapons of mass destruction attack at locations where the materials had not yet been found.

Rachel said she abhorred the idea that the plan had been foiled.

"What if everything that we have interdicted so far is just the tip of a very nasty iceberg?" she asked.

I asked her to elaborate on a scenario that still worked without the simultaneous attacks on the ports. She answered that everyone knew that delivery of a nuclear weapon by missile and cyber attacks could, by themselves, bring the nation's economy and defense to their knees within thirty minutes. Even the Director of the National Security Agency, the NSA, has admitted in a public forum that there is no adequate defense against a cyber attack.

"Besides," she continued, "Look at how much we depend on our satellites for communication and weather prediction and whatnot else. Anti-satellite weapons of Russia and China are sufficient to wipe those assets out in the same thirty minutes that it will take an Intercontinental Ballistic Missile to fly from Russia to the U.S."

I had to agree with her, but I maintained that we in the Agency could do nothing about our defense capabilities other than analyze foreign capabilities and perform net assessments. Our defense capabilities would be ready or not in the event of a general war, period. I said that we should look at the situation not from the standpoint of what we could not do, but from the standpoint of what we could do. It was all about the art of the possible. Our advantage might be in coming up with a countermeasure that could work in plenty of time to render the threat defunct. Given what we had said about the current regime in Russia, it would not matter if we could cause regime change. The plan would be executed even if the Russian government was annihilated.

"So we have to look at the haystack as a whole, and then we must find the needle in it? Who has enough experience and brainpower to enlighten us on what our target is?" Rachel was exasperated but trying to catalyze some constructive action. She simply could not be cynical, and she was by no means shocked by what we were uncovering together.

I had been considering this very question myself, and I told Rachel that she should pack for a three-day excursion to Phoenix, Arizona. I said that the temperature was going to be warm enough for her to pack her swimsuit and shorts and summer shoes. She brightened right up at the thought. We would be visiting a very old friend who might help instruct us on the history behind the transition from the USSR to the Russian Federation. The man was an old Russia hand named Benjamin Sweeney, an Agency legend during the Cold War and one of the architects of the world of the post-Soviet Union. I made the call, and Ben Sweeney said he would be delighted to see us poolside at his place in Phoenix. He gave me his address and directions. Better still, he told me that he would have me picked up at Sky Harbor and taken to a place where we could talk without the microphones that had been planted all over his house by the Agency counterintelligence people. He said we should stay where his driver recommended.

Rachel asked me, "Anderson, why would your friend's driver make the recommendation?"

"Don't think it's odd. The driver is most certainly ex-Agency and works closely with his boss."

Our flight from LA to Phoenix was short. It was worth the trip to see the green paradise of the Sun Valley spring into view and extend for miles. Ben's driver, Hal Metcalf, met us at the baggage claim area and drove west out of Phoenix proper to a town named Wickenburg, where Hal showed us the motel at which we were to stay. We checked in and unloaded our belongings at the motel with Hal's assistance, and then we changed into our summer clothes. When we were ready Hal drove us to the Wickenburg Country Club. On the veranda sat Ben Sweeney with an ice tea, looking out over the golf course with its desert motif. The golf course had been designed to fit right into the desert landscape, and its well-manicured greenery on both fairways and greens indicated there was plenty of water even at the height of summer. The sun was bright but not oppressive.

Ben looked up and said, "Let's move inside so we don't get sunburned." He then rose and threw his arms around me and we hugged each other like the mentor and his protégé that we were. Our embrace was long and soulfelt. He put me at arm's length to look me over. He also admired Rachel by eyeing her unabashedly from head to foot and gave me a wink of approval. He invited Hal to join us for our discussions.

Ben Sweeney had recruited me into the Agency and groomed me as his successor. He had been caught in one of the Reductions in Force that beset the old Russia hands when the lion and lamb lay down together and peace was breaking out all over the world. Ben was as sharp as he ever was, and he shook his head over an Agency that no longer cultivated linguists, that relied entirely on computers and that placed too much emphasis on the interchangeability of agents. He was a living link to Stephenson and the so-called cowboys of the original school, whose legacy reached back to the swashbuckling days of the Office of Special Services and World War II.

I saw that Rachel was looking over Ben with the same curiosity he had shown her. He had always been an unusual man physically as well as mentally. For example, for the last sixty years Ben shaved his head every morning, and it shone in the interior light of the club house where we sat by a window looking out on the veranda and into the palms.

"Let me guess," Ben said, after introductions, "you want to know what is actually happening with all the weapons of mass destruction caches you are discovering? I thought as much. Further, you wish to know whether everything traces back to a Russian connection. Well, of course, you would."

With that Ben suggested that we order our lunches and drinks and prepare for a long afternoon's discussion. Ben looked at Rachel before he began talking.

"You are not Agency, but you are working with Anderson here on sensitive operations that have no names and no acknowledgment. Brave woman! Anderson thinks very highly of you, or you would not be here."

Rachel smiled uneasily and shifted in her chair, but she did not take her eyes off of his.

"I don't have to tell you that if you are not what you seem to be to him, you would be in very grave danger even now at this table. I am going to trust you until you prove untrustworthy, and then God help us all. By the way, you remind me a lot of someone very close to me, by which I mean me. Listen up, and ask questions at any point. This garrulous old man has a few tales to tell, and sometimes I get carried away so that people wonder how everything connects. Any questions? No? Anderson? No. Hal? No. Okay, let me start back in the Middle East five decades ago in the thick of the Cold War. We had a rough game with rules. Nuclear winter was a reality as opposed to the disinformation campaign historians now call it."

Ben's stories were like the best spy fiction, only they had the ring of truth, and you knew by their details that they came from a man who fought on the front lines of the Cold War that was not only cold, but hot as well. Ben had seen suicide bombing evolve from being a Russian innovation over centuries-old Islamic tradition to being the front line tactic of Islamists around the world. Ben said that we should consider that the influence went both ways. When the major powers were plotting the extinction of humankind through Mutual Assured Destruction, the USSR and the U.S., and, to a lesser degree, the People's Republic of China were doing the global version of suicide bombing writ large. Pull the idea inside out, and you find that the USSR had allies without portfolio and without national boundaries who potentially outnumbered all other denizens of the planet. Their central focus was the Middle East, and for good reason. If the infrastructure of the twin oil and gas pipelines of the Kingdom of Saudi Arabia were attacked and put offline for six months, the world economy would crash. Why was Russia scrambling to shore up its holdings of gold, making common cause with China and India, creating a banking system that was the counterpoint to Western banks, and soldering relationships with as many other countries as it could? Russia was building an alternative universe against a time when the West no longer existed. Ben ticked on his fingers all the horrific scenarios that we had considered including weapons of mass destruction, cyber and anti-sat, both together and separately as threats. He went beyond all these to muse on what group of people might have the vision and experience to plan and execute an attack with the scope and ferocity that was implied by the weapons of mass destruction at all the key U.S. ports.

Through all this, Anderson and Rachel nodded, riveted by the authority of Sweeney's bearing, tone and voice. They knew he was not to be trifled with.

For a while, Ben remained silent, and he cautioned anyone at the table from jumping on any of the usual conspiracy bandwagons. He said what he knew was not theory but fact. He declared that the United States could never have survived the humiliation of defeat that Russians felt when the USSR ceased to exist.

"One day, they were the second greatest power on earth trying hard to be the greatest. They felt that history was on their side. Marx and Lenin had told them so. Then suddenly without a shot being fired, they had been defeated. The enemy had breached their walls and covered their country with commercialism that they did not understand and deeply resented. How would Americans have felt to have capitalism destroyed and dumped on the ash heap of history? How would we have felt to have Communists set up communes throughout what used to be fifty states? What would we have thought about living with what Winston Churchill had called shared misery? We would not have fought any more than the citizens of the former Soviet Union fought. Would we have resisted after twenty-five years under the heel of conquerors? Who knows?"

"In the longer view of time, twenty-five years is a very short interval, not enough to erase memory, and certainly not enough to eliminate chains of ideas and powerful friendships. Change the name of the USSR to the Russian Empire that still has all the weapons of mass destruction of its predecessor, and what do you have? You have a history of barbaric plunder that goes back to the Rus pirates of the Ninth Century. What we hear from the

Russian Federation today is the same rhetoric that came out of the mouth of geopolitical pundits who worked for Alexander III or out of the mouth of Khrushchev."

"Rachel, please take my word for some of this background—I will give you titles you can read that have not yet been transposed to the Internet. You might smile to think that the Internet itself is an invention that largely came to life after the demise of the USSR. In fact, cyber warfare as we know it is a different animal entirely than the electronic warfare of the Cold War era. The USSR had the best electronic warfare in the world then. Now the U.S. is looking at a coup potential that in seconds could bring the country to its knees."

Ben named the names and told the stories of Soviet and Russian agents against whom he had worked in the Middle East, in Eastern Europe, and in Asia.

"Russia had provided the global vision that drove all their actions, and Moscow Center maneuvered people and money all over the world under direct, continuous control. Nothing was left to chance. The U.S. could count on an interaction that was so tightly orchestrated that, from a particular level of view, everything in the monotonous accumulation of moves and countermoves was one big picture. Whether you worked against Andropov or Primakov, and no matter the politics of the Kremlin, you were working against one entity, not multitudes."

Ben paused because he had come to his central point. "For all the changes over a quarter of a century, the enduring threat remains. We called the enemy the Communists, and they still exist. The real enemy can be found in the competition of nation-states struggling for survival and mastery across the world. Any player not at that level cannot understand the game. Focus on a few weapons of mass destruction in ports, and you lose the perspective that delivers the whole plan."

"Through the transition from the USSR to the Russia of today, one man kept a single map on his office wall. It was a map inverted from our way of looking at the world. It was oriented with Russia at its center at the bottom. Looking up and therefore south, the man extended pieces of yarn tied to pins from Moscow to all the places where his agents operated. The map of Russia was colorized so that the growth of Russia from a small group of tribes on the Volga and Moscow Rivers expanded in rings to encompass all the regions from the Baltic Sea to the Bering Strait and from the North Pole to the borders of China, India and Iran."

"I saw a picture of that map in a newspaper during the waning days of the USSR," I added reflectively to show that I remembered and was part of Ben's memory.

"The map still exists today, though the man Primakov is now dead. Members of his coterie still live in Moscow. Their protégés write the scripts for the current regime, who are no more and no less than puppets to their vision. Things have become more complicated since the fall of the Berlin Wall because so many of their plans have worked so well with America blinded and its efforts diffused by the plan. Their triumph was what we call the Global War on Terror. You might as well try to change the course of the Earth around the Sun as to change the minds of the men behind this vision." Ben stopped and asked our waiter to refill our drinks.

"Ben," said Rachel, "Your picture is complete, but perhaps in that is a defect. May I proceed?" Ben smiled and gestured that the stage was entirely hers.

Rachel said that Ben had ended where he began, talking of history as determined so that no human agency could change it. With respect but with rising fervor in a steady voice, she said she differed with that view. As she saw it, humankind could chart its own course. Individual pockets of people, no matter how large, could never press a vision on all people. History had repeatedly shown that personal visions do not prevail. She quoted from Lord Byron's poem about Ozymandias, King of Kings, wherein only a ruin remained of the vaunted empire of the long-deceased boaster. She used the example of King Canute, who tried to stop the waves from dancing with his command. She talked about the failure of individual rulers including Napoleon and Hitler to impose their visions on the world. She colored as she spoke, and Ben seemed to be impressed with her fire and courage. When she had finished, Ben looked her right in the eye and said, "Brava!" But Rachel would not be patronized, though she nodded slightly to acknowledge Ben's praise. Seizing upon her opportunity, she asked him what he would do to get to the bottom of the current plot against the U.S. and stop it.

It was mid afternoon, and because of the descending Arizona sun, shadows were crawling gradually towards the clubhouse. The clubhouse was empty except for us four and the waitress, who seemed to be preoccupied with the cash register. Ben said that if he were in my shoes, he would find the man who was being groomed to replace the current leader of the gray men and assassinate him. Russia would not be able to replace him for ten to twenty years. He said, "With the connection between the gray men and the current government broken, Russia would be adrift. No one would acknowledge the importance of the man whom he would kill. Their power depends on no one knowing where it comes from."

"Powerful people," Ben continued, "know where their power resides and all the strands that lead to it. Power is like the strings of yarn that the old spymaster laid out from Moscow to all the corners of the globe. Anderson, find the man who was programmed to take control of that map and those strings, make wise plans to take him out, and you will have the key to scotching Russia's rampant rise."

"Yes, sir. I'll find him and take him out. You can count on that." I spoke with conviction, and Ben knew that I would follow through. Rachel rose in her seat with pride to see that I was now committed. Hal rose from his chair and moved to stand at ease opposite to his seated boss while Sweeney rounded out the conversation.

"Now I am going to insist that you take the evening flight back to LA. Your tickets have been arranged. Hal will take you back to Sky Harbor after you stop to pick up your belongings at the motel. It is far too dangerous for you to stay in Sun Valley knowing what you know. Your early departure will be a sign to whoever is watching us that you could not get what you wanted from me. That is just as well since we never had the chance to meet."

To emphasize the importance of these words, Ben made eye contact with each person in turn to be sure they had heard him.

"There are no surveillance cameras in this clubhouse or on any of the roads into this place or out of it. When you arrive at Sky Harbor, you will be observed to depart disappointed. Please try your best not to be jolly. You came and you wasted your time eating lunch at a golf course where no one else was eating and your contact failed to appear." With that, Ben Sweeney asked to be excused to go to the john. When he returned, we were on the way to our motel, and that afternoon we flew, glum and disheartened, back to LA and our boring old safe house.

Rachel broke out a bottle of cold Chablis when we had unpacked our things at the safe house. She poured two glasses of wine and angled her head towards the door to the porch that overlooked the Pacific Ocean. There we reviewed what we had learned from Ben Sweeney in detail. Rachel said that she liked Ben because of his perspective and because he went to the heart of the matter. I told her that Ben was simply the best we had, and I loved him like a son does his father. Rachel replied that she saw the resemblance except that I did not shave all my hair off. With a chuckle, she reminded me that the last person she saw with all his hair shaved off was pictured in all the tabloids in the world and lost all his money.

We laughed in good humor, and then we returned to discussing our mission. Ben had given us direction. We knew what we were looking for, but we did not have a name. How would we get that name? That was the question. We would have to sleep on the question to see whether we could derive the answer from our sleep. Rachel suggested that sex was the best soporific for both of us, and when we finished our glasses of wine, she took my hand and we retired to the bedroom. We decided to strip and shower together before we went to bed, and when we dried off after our shower, we decided to give each other a massage. We were both very tense from our encounter with Ben, and our muscles were knotted and sore. We were getting good at massages, so by the time she had done me and I had done her, we decided it was time to do each other. Rachel had a new look when I found her eyes below me. I had somehow gained in her estimation because of my relationship with Ben. She had also grown in my esteem because she had so daringly held forth about the burden of determinism. I suppose she saw that she was esteemed as well as loved, and she colored in appreciation. Women have so many ways to communicate with men, and I was learning that Rachel knew how to use them all to both of our advantage.

Tonight was a kind of triumph of the imagination, but we saw to it that it was a triumph of our physicality as well. We were not determined; we were free. Yet I was finding that the more I let her fly, the more I needed to fly with her. Was that really freedom? I asked Rachel the question as I stroked her breast and rubbed her shaven pubis softly. I ran my hand between her thighs up to the wet, hot place where my fingers lingered and moved gently in a vibrato that left the tone of her moaning in my ears. As she arched and rubbed herself up and down the length of my finger, she said she knew the answer to my question. I was sucking her nipple at the moment, but when I tried to raise my head to ask her what the answer was, she gently pushed my head back to its task and ruffled my hair.

"You know the answer," she said, followed by rising moans. "Nnnngh. Ummm." That was when we shifted to another key entirely, and I was in her and she was flying high but below me, and I was flying lightly over her, our wings touching. Her thighs spread wide and her heels were now dug into my behind as she pushed me into her from the back. I saw what she meant, and our passion overtook us. Kissing and fondling, pushing and pulling, sliding and trying to hold and squeeze, we were not two humans, but one loving entity entirely absorbed with itself. She both held me inside her at the hilt and opened deep inside of her like a cave. I grew to the size of her endless canal and at the tip, I flowered as she flowered. I rushed into her receiving softness, arching and feeling her buckle upwards, then quiver all along me as my spasms told her that we were in synchrony and harmony, both coming together once, and then again. We held our positions against the odds, and I felt her squeeze me like an internal hug, and I responded by growing so large that her black eyes widened and then closed tight in ecstasy. I let her descend, and as I slipped to the side, her eyes opened to say, "Thank you." And then, "Let's do that again, right now." Our fingers began the slow and tender explorations, and voila, the raven-eyed lady stirred, and I stirred answering her. We took off again, and we soared.

Rachel Plays in Deutschland

Rachel and I were enjoying a Rhine River cruise with the picturesque castles visible on cliff tops as we glided by. Our tourist cover was perfect for our getting a little international R&R while we prepared for our new mission. It helped that I was fluent in German, but in Germany the best passport is traveling with a beautiful woman, so Rachel was the secret of my safe passage. The men could not keep their eyes off of her, and the haughty hausfrau stares would have felt threatening to anyone who did not have Rachel's natural disposition to ignore potential catty and jealous rivals. Our mission was designed by ourselves, not by the Agency. So we were deniable to my masters and without safety nets or backups of any kind.

Our return to LA from lunch in Wickenburg, Arizona, was followed by a week of research and strategy to determine the best approach to our target. We got lucky by discovering that a former agent of Russian intelligence was in a hospital in Dusseldorf dying of a now-pandemic problem among former intelligence agents, radionuclide poisoning. The Russian Federation as a practice terminated their rogues with extreme prejudice. They sent two goons to administer the radionuclides in liquid form. Then they left their victim to discover his or her ailment and die in agony.

Our target, the Russian intelligence agent who was dying in Dusseldorf, was a native of Germany who had spent his entire operational life working as Moscow's chief liaison to Islamist terrorist cells throughout the Middle East. He was rumored to be a protégé of Primakov himself, and before his fall from grace he was being groomed as Primakov's successor. I counted our odds of reaching him before he died as fifty/fifty and our chances of getting anything useful out of him as twenty/eighty. Even though his open interview with Der Spiegel indicated that he had left the pale of Russian intelligence, spies like him were notoriously loyal when it came to divulging deep secrets even with death a certainty in the near term. Our plan was to see the man, ask him a few questions, get a few answers from him, and then get away before the ever-watchful FSB networks destroyed us. My secret weapon was Rachel, and she was looking even more ravishing than usual. Our plan had to work, but I did not want to put too much pressure on my protégé.

"This Rhineland is a fairyland," she said. "It's difficult to imagine Hitler holding sway here."

"How so, Rachel?"

"It's so green and well kept. How did the princes manage to get all those large stones up the crags to make the castles? It's a long way down to fetch water and food in the valley below. Do you suppose the fairy tales are right that the birds flew up with the food to feed them?" Rachel liked to play 'suppose…'. It was her form of comic relief before a mission. She was like a little girl with her father, laughing and pointing to what she liked and speaking in excited, girlish tones. I enjoyed watching her, and sometimes I felt old enough in experience to be her father. Given my looks, if I were her father, her mother would have to be some combination of the Virgin Mary and a latter day Greta Garbo.

Finding the hospital was no problem. To my surprise and delight, our target was in an unguarded room. We did not even have to sign anything to get inside to see him. There he sat slumping to one side with his head shaven in his hospital bed, a drip feeding his arm. Ewald Krueger seemed so tired that his head was lolling slightly and he had dark circles under his eyes, but he brightened up immediately when he saw Rachel, and I knew we were going to get what we came for. Rachel might have asked Herr Krueger to climb to the top of the Brandenburg Gate or to swim the Rhine in full armor. No task would be too difficult for this old warhorse to please one of the loveliest of the Lorelei. She simply said that she was a freelance reporter interested in asking a few questions about his fascinating life as a spy. I did the translating for what the pair said to each other, and I was, therefore, invisible to Ewald, who did not spare me a second glance. My presence was a foregone conclusion rather than a threat. The man was wholly fixated on Rachel. Because she had memorized our questions, I did not have to prompt her even once.

The first question she asked the spy was, "Is it true that you are the protégé of Yevgeny Primakov?" He answered that he had learned much from Primakov, but it might be presumptuous to infer that he was the spymaster's protégé. Rachel followed up by asking him to name one other spy who had done so much for the Russian intelligence in the Levant and the Middle East generally.

Krueger's ego now kicked in. "No," he said, he knew of no one who had done so much for so many Jihadists across that region and in the world. He said that his access was his knowledge of Arabic dialects and Islamic customs. He could always provide what the terrorist cells needed by way of money, supplies and logistics. No one else could do that. Rachel stoically heard the man out, though she told me later she was thunderstruck by the man's revelations. He was confessing to all the crimes we had suspected. At the time, I was impressed by her grace under fire.

Rachel pressed him by asking whether he worked according to a plan or program or as a freelancer, like herself. Ewald did not hesitate to say that from the beginning the plan for the Islamist movement was designed by Primakov, and it was brilliant. What other alliance could offer unlimited violence, a people who were willing to fight to the death for their cause and worldwide presence? The Islamist movement started well before the Berlin Wall fell, he said, but Primakov had provided the kindling and the initial fire. By the time Communism fell, the Russia-inspired Islamic movement had shaken the world.

Rachel saw an angle and followed her instincts. She asked Krueger, "Did you see no contradiction between a world dominated by Communists and a world dominated by Islamists?"

Nodding his head but keeping his eyes locked on hers, he said that was a natural question, but Primakov's genius provided the linkage between the two movements. Krueger told her, "Communism needed renewal at the time that the Wall fell down. Islam could keep the geopolitical vision whole until Communism could rise from the ashes and triumph over all. Historical determinism would prevail in the end."

Rachel cocked her head and squinted her eyes as if to say, "Tell me more."

So Krueger said, "True Communists know that history takes many turns like a mighty river, but it has an eventual course and reckoning. True believers are few, but history will prove them right. I have always believed this. I converted to Islam and memorized the Quran. I want to be buried as a Moslem. Yet I was born a Communist and will die a true believer. I see no contradiction in that." Krueger was in a confessional mood, and he wanted Rachel's absolution. She instinctually understood the message in his imploring eyes.

"Was it true that the Russian intelligence apparatus poisoned you with Strontium? And why did they want to do that?" she asked him.

"Two agents from Moscow asked me to fly to Berlin for an urgent meeting. It was a trap, and I knew it. I always enter a trap because you can learn so many things that way. So I went to the meeting, had tea and cookies there, and I received word that Primakov was no longer in charge of my activities. They said that I could expect to receive new orders almost immediately. For the time being, I was supposed to put everything on hold. I objected because I had so many things going on, a big plan with many moving pieces and parts. I was the center of all actions. If I suddenly stopped everything, the plan would be in jeopardy. The two men laughed and said that nothing was that important in the long view of things. They said that, like my mentor, I thought too much of my own abilities. They left like the bureaucrats that they were. I hated them as much for what they were as for what they said. I knew that the situation in Moscow had changed, and I became frightened for Primakov and for all his people as well as for myself." The broken spy became flushed with excitement and hatred as he spoke these words.

"And that is why you went to Der Spiegel for your interview?"

"I did not call for the interview until I knew for certain that I had been poisoned. Now I had only a few weeks, the doctors said, to live. My insides were all being cooked by the nuclear radiation. Primakov had not done this to me. I tried to contact him, but he would not see me. He said it was too dangerous." The spy's tone changed now because he was talking about his beloved mentor, whom he admired.

"He said that the little men who now run Russia poisoned me. He thanked me for all that I had done and said that now I was on my own. That was when I decided to make a statement for history and called the editor of Der Spiegel." The old spy sank back and looked straight into Rachel's eyes as if she could somehow give him absolution for the unforgivable thing that he had done. She realized that she had to bring the interview to a swift conclusion.

"So what happened with the plan that you were executing? Did that just go away somehow? Is someone else executing the plan now? If so, who would that be?"

Krueger laughed so hard that he coughed. "I did not know it, but the plan had begun to run itself. All the cells and materials were in place. The plan was much too large and complicated to have it collapse because of one man's absence. What if I had been killed? The design of the plan accounted for that. It still does. Now no one from Moscow needs to execute. No one from Moscow can stop the plan, no matter how they try."

Rachel breathed deeply, blinked her beautiful eyes, and went for the jackpot question. She asked, "So how will this plan that is so big and so complex execute itself?"

Krueger looked at Rachel as if he recognized something about her that he did not like. He began coughing uncontrollably. She tried to give him some water, and he knocked her proffered glass onto the floor, breaking the glass. Krueger began to bleed from his nose profusely, and he buckled over and coughed up blood. I handed Krueger a napkin, which he took. He dabbed at his mouth and nose, his uncontrollable hacking coughs filling the air. The old spy suddenly sat up, looking as if he had received a shock. His head twitched violently, and he reached up as if to contain a pain in his cranium. He collapsed. His heartbeat monitor began to whine and I saw that his heartbeat had flatlined. His pulse monitor showed failure too. I got Rachel's attention and signaled that it was time for us to go. I left the room with her following close behind me.

As we walked down the corridor, a nurse and an orderly ran by us on their way to Krueger's room. The nurse turned back to see who we were, but she did not get more than a quarter view of our faces. She was far too busy with her patient's emergency to raise a general alarm. We were outside on the other side of the street from the hospital when the police arrived with their sirens sounding and their lights flashing. Rachel and I ducked into a coffee shop and went straight to the restrooms to apply light disguises. We used the rear exit and met in the half-street behind the coffee shop. I took her hand and with my free hand, I extracted a tourist map that I shook open. We walked slowly discussing what we would see next on our tour of this memorable city. When we reached the main street again, I hailed the first taxi that I saw. We began planning our new odyssey of escape. We were not only fleeing the German police and intelligence service, but we were also fleeing the long, grasping tentacles of the Russian intelligence organization.

We couldn't look like we're fleeing because that would be a dead giveaway. We needed somewhere definite to go, a destination. So Rachel and I went to visit Auschwitz to commiserate about the Holocaust. We followed the Jewish memorials looking for evidence of Rachel's fictional German relatives, the Blomfelds, who had been exterminated by the Nazis during World War II. We watched for surveillance, and we were careful not to make ourselves stand out by our dress or behavior. Rachel did not wear any makeup, and she wore her hair up in a chignon. I wore my professorial spectacles and my nondescript brown jacket with the leather sewn on the elbows. The professor and his bereaved Jewish wife spent three days reviewing every detail of one of the saddest episodes in human history. Then on the fourth day, we took a second Rhine cruise, this time as honeymooners wending our way to the Swiss Alps for skiing. From Switzerland, we flew back to the USA and to LA. We arrived at our safe house at the beach with a new idea, and we hit the ground running with that.

Meanwhile, we read that Krueger had died. Nearly everything that he had told us, he had already told to Der Spiegel, but the magazine's editor must have kept the material for publication at the spy's death. So we were a few days ahead of the curve, but now the whole world knew what we discovered beside what turned out to be the spy's deathbed. No mention was made in the eulogy and reprise in Der Spiegel about Krueger's last visitors. As we had planned, our visit never actually happened.

Rachel said that our traveling to Germany was like a trip to fairyland. I did not contradict her, but I rather thought it was like a trip to a country-wide madhouse. Only when we arrived safely in Switzerland did I believe that we might be free from repercussions. For me, going into Germany this time and coming out again alive was reminiscent of what my mentor had said about the bad old days of the Cold War. Dante had Vergil as his guide through hell in his Inferno. I had Rachel as my consort through the hell that was Deutschland.

Neither Rachel nor I could sympathize much with Ewald Krueger. He had set up the nightmare scenario that we were trying to unravel and interdict. He and his mentor had done unspeakable things in their conflation and confusion of Communism and Islamism. In the end, Krueger's enormous ego had provided us with a glimpse into his mind and methods. I felt both overwhelmed and frustrated by what we had learned in Germany. We now knew that the power struggle between the new Russian Federation politicians and the old USSR Cold War heroes would be the pretext for Russia claiming no culpability for the attacks that had been planned against the U.S. The attack would be called a rogue effort by Russia, which would reap all the benefits of the attack they fomented in the first place.

Ewald Krueger spent his life as a spy taking instructions from a government that cashiered him as a reward for his service. Now he and those he served would become scapegoats in the blame game following the weapons of mass destruction attacks against the U.S. Ironically, our country might find the new politicians useful in defusing some of the plan, but that would be up to the Agency and, ultimately, the President. Meanwhile, teams in all the agencies were sifting through operational data to discover the elements of the grand plan that applied to LA.

If the first thread leading to the plot began to unravel in San Pedro, the last thread leading to the whole plot's unraveling, we thought, might be found in the port of LA and Long Beach.

"What goes around comes around," I whispered in Rachel's ear, but by that point we were too involved in our life-affirming activities. Her only comment was a low moan. I could not agree more.

Rachel Clandestine

Rachel and I were back in the City of the Angels where I first found her. We were focusing on a proximate threat whose dimensions we could only guess at. The short version is that weapons of mass destruction materials and beaucoup explosives had been planted in a shipping container, a warehouse or a commercial storage facility somewhere in the Los Angeles-Long Beach area. We only supposed that the stuff was not in San Pedro where we had found the chemical weapons and explosives that signaled big trouble for the U.S.

It made no sense to us that the terrorists would have put two weapons of mass destruction packages virtually on top of each other. For security, surely they would have put the second package somewhere else. It also made sense that the terrorists would not have doubled their chemical weapons. In all likelihood, they would have used biological, radionuclide or nuclear, but the Nuclear Emergency Support Team folks had scoured the entire area, including San Pedro, and nuclear was ruled out.

So we were left with a nasty biological warfare package, and depending on the microbes or viruses, explosives would be minimal. Some form of sprayer would be optimal, but we figured that small aerosol units might be used at airports or malls with the same ultimate effects as airborne sprayers—infection, death, hysteria, and chaos, and not necessarily in that order.

I did some investigating about the best possible biological weapon for a terrorist to use in the greater LA area. I called Bill Caxton, an old friend of mine at the United States Army Medical Research Institute for Infectious Diseases, and he told me the best person to ask about such biological warfare matters was a former bio-warrior now making his living as a veterinarian in Riverside, California. His name was Harold Marriott, DVM.

I told Rachel that we were going for a picnic the next day in Riverside. We would arrive in Riverside early, eat lunch and then drop by Dr. Marriott's veterinary clinic in the early afternoon. I had already called his office, and his assistant had said Dr. Marriott would have an hour open just after lunch to talk. Rachel packed us an outstanding picnic of duck sandwiches with lettuce and a cooler with two bottles of white wine.

Marriott's Veterinary Clinic was different from what I expected. It was located on fifteen acres of prime land, with a stable, a kennel and an open-air terrarium where giant turtles roamed or chomped on fresh lettuce. There were no pretensions about the business. Inside the door, people sat with their pets awaiting the attentions of interns. The sign above the main desk read: "No Scorpions, Tarantulas, Gila Monsters or Rattle Snakes." Another large sign read: "Take Horses Directly to the Stables. Take Cattle and Bison to the Small Pasture." Just after the receptionist announced us to the vet, he bounded into the reception area and said we should all go to the stable because he had a troubled pregnancy to attend to.

In the stable while Dr. Marriott performed extraction birth of a filly from a palomino mare, he spoke nonstop about what he would do if he were a terrorist trying to wreak havoc on Greater LA. He was so animated about the subject, it was clear that he had thought a lot about this clear and present danger with no tasking to do so from his institute. When he had reviewed his dozen top biological warfare favorites one by one, including ebola and smallpox, he said that—definitively the best agent to use was Venezuelan Equine Encephalitis or VEE, which, though named for horse infection, was perhaps the deadliest agent known to man. Rachel and I were appalled by the veterinarian and scientist's casual delight at the thought of such a lethal biological agent. With a beaming smile, he said that with westerly offshore winds prevailing, VEE would kill every human in the region within seven days. No one would have the time for proper lab work because the virus worked so fast. He said this while cradling the newborn filly before laying it gently on its legs on the stable floor.

While observing the newborn gain its footing and edge towards its mother, the vet went on to say that because VEE was fatal to horses, no one thought about it much as an agent to use against humans, but the bio-weaponeers liked it well enough. Before 1963, the USSR had quite a testing program going near the Sea of Azov. The U.S. also had a program in Utah, but that was halted by the biological weapons accords. No one knew what happened to the Soviet program, but some evidence suggested that it had migrated to Iraq and Syria and continued unabated. Dr. Marriott said that he had personally traced the best people in that arena from Russia to Syria. Some were still in Syria in spite of all the trouble the country was having. After the second Gulf War, Syria was the only remaining source for that virus outside of stock samples in Russia, the U.S. and possibly China, which had gotten its samples from either

Russia or Syria. If someone had been able to smuggle out VEE from the Syrian bio labs during recent years, the samples could well be sitting in any of the ports around LA.

Rachel asked him whether anything special had to be done to keep the stock active, what had to be done to make the samples airborne and what kind of expertise was necessary to deploy the VEE biological weapon. To these questions, the vet shook his head in amazement. He said that the sample size would probably be large, but a small refrigerator unit would accommodate enough to destroy the population of greater LA. For the best results, the sample should be dispensed through aerosol nozzles, like crop dusting nozzles, at around five-thousand feet along the Pacific coastline two miles offshore. The only training that would be required would be crop dusting experience on how to load the samples into the applicator units, knowledge of how to release the samples through the nozzles and how to evade getting in the way of the biological warfare cloud that you would produce. "Of course," he said, "terrorists often do not expect to survive a mission, and in this case, the probability of surviving VEE was next to nil."

As a wild stab, I asked whether the vet knew of any suspicious cases of VEE during the last two years in Southern California. Dr. Marriott replied that there may have been such a case out near Ocotillo around eighteen months ago. He had been called down to investigate the sudden demise of an entire herd of thirty prime horses. He said that he diagnosed the deaths as caused by VEE. He would not ordinarily have offered that diagnosis, but he had ruled out all other possibilities and that left the zebra.

Rachel asked the vet what he meant by 'the zebra', and he smiled and answered that every doctor of animals or humans keeps in the back of his or her mind possibilities that are most unusual but may present symptoms at any time. He said that most diseases are horses, and you can tell them by the usual signs. Some sound and look like horses, but they are exotics, similar to the usual but differentiated enough to be zebras with black and white stripes. He asked her whether she would recognize a zebra when she saw one. She said she would. He said that then she would understand that he had seen a zebra in Ocotillo and had reported the matter to his institute as a precaution. Until today, he said, he had received no feedback on the matter. When I asked the vet whether he could give me the name and address of his point of contact in Ocotillo, Dr. Marriott said that he could do so, but it would not do us any good because the man died two days after he had made contact.

The vet mused that he was probably lucky not to have succumbed to VEE himself on account of his visit to Ocotillo. With a shrug, he waved both his arms, "Well, no matter. Here I am to tell you about it!"

I thanked the cheery vet for his time and expert opinion. I told him that I might need to confer with him again as I pursued my investigations. He welcomed that opportunity and gave me his personal cell phone number. As we left the stable, we saw Dr. Marriott talking gently to the mare and her newborn as if they were humans under his care.

While we drove, I called the Sheriff of Ocotillo and talked with him for thirty minutes on speaker phone about what he thought had happened to the thirty horses and their owner eighteen months ago. He said that he was mystified about the occurrence but thought the cause must have been anthrax. All the dead horses had been buried with bulldozers in a common grave. The human corpse was cremated at the request of his relatives and buried in their family plot in Ocotillo. I asked the Sheriff if he knew of any nearby private airports where a small plane could be equipped with crop dusting gear. He said that he knew of one such airport, and he gave me its name and the number of its proprietor. He did not know why anyone needed crop dusters in Ocotillo since the small town was all desert and was likely to remain so for the foreseeable future. I thanked the Sheriff for his time. I told him that I might just drive out to see a few people in Ocotillo someday soon. I said I was not a reporter, so he need not worry about adverse publicity. He replied that he did not care one way or the other about publicity. After news of the fatal horse incident hit the wires of the Associated Press, the Sheriff did not figure on anyone raising horses in Ocotillo anytime soon.

On a whim, I asked the Sheriff if any other suspicious deaths had occurred in or near Ocotillo from any cause during the weeks surrounding the horse incident. The Sheriff seemed to be consulting his official diary for a few minutes, and then he said that there had been a murder by gunshot wound to the head out near the airport before the report of the horse incident. He figured that was most likely drugs or trafficking because that airport had a reputation for both. When Rachel heard this, she gave me a sign that we should end the call and talk.

I let Rachel put together what she had learned as we drove north to LA. She reviewed the data we had been given today item by item, and then she began to tie the data to what I had discovered during my in-and-out sojourn in Mexico.

She asked, "Would it be possible for a small plane to do this? Perhaps something like the one you chartered for your Mexican op for the VEE mission?"

"That would be unlikely because of the nozzles that would be required. You are onto something with a little different twist. A small plane could ferry a terrorist team to Ocotillo where they could transfer to a crop duster. The problem would then be to fly the plane to a point in LA and dispense the VEE as the vet prescribed." I saw the possibilities but needed to work out the particulars.

"If the VEE had been tested at Ocotillo, two things must be true," she said. "First, a sufficient sample of VEE had to be available to load onto the crop duster at the airport. Second, a terrorist team had to be present to dispense the VEE from that plane as a practice run for the main terrorist attack against LA." I nodded. What she said made perfect sense. Operationally, both things would have to be accounted for.

"I agree with you on both points. An airport that dealt in drugs and human trafficking would be the perfect venue. My only problem with this whole line of thinking is that any airplane that was used as a dispenser for VEE was likely to be a death trap. In that event, we should find evidence of mysterious deaths." I became excited by this possibility, and Rachel caught my excitement while searching for a way forward.

"You are assuming that the practice team remained alive after performing their mission. What if they had been summarily executed or that they had died of the VEE just after the proof of concept and had been buried in the desert, as if they had been involved in a drug deal gone badly?"

"What you're saying might be true, but until we rule out evidence to the contrary, we should pursue the possibility that someone involved in the spraying had died from mysterious causes and that we could find him or her through searching open sources. One of the problems with such a search is the enormous volume of killings that were the direct result of drug dealing and human trafficking. At present, I don't know how we can winnow out the killings that we are looking for from the rest."

That evening in the safe house, Rachel and I did our independent searches of suspicious deaths and unsolved homicides on both sides of the Mexican border around the time of the Ocotillo horse deaths. In the open literature, three deaths fit our search criteria. A woman pilot, an Air Force veteran age thrity-four, had died at the public dump in Otay Mesa. She had died from a single gunshot wound to the head. Her death appeared to be an execution, but the woman had no known connection to criminal elements. She was a free-lance aviator and pilot trainer with an excellent record of flight safety. The other two deaths, both Middle Eastern males around twenty-five years old, had occurred along drug mule trails meandering east and south from San Diego through the desert to the Mexican border. The bodies showed no signs of violence but did show indications of some unknown disease.

I asked Rachel to tell me what she deduced from the evidence. She said that one compelling scenario was that the female pilot had brought three persons across the border clandestinely and landed at Ocotillo, where two of the three completed the mission and, upon their return to Ocotillo, went south on foot to return to Mexico. The third passenger took the female pilot in her car, probably at gunpoint, to Otay Mesa, killed her and left her car at the dump. That person probably just walked across the border into Mexico. Rachel guessed that the police had taken fingerprints that were latent in the deceased pilot's car. Perhaps the fingerprints would be helpful to the investigation. She mused that the person who found the two bodies in the desert might be helpful, but then again, perhaps not since the incident had occurred eighteen months ago.

I said that by her scenario, one of the two dead Middle Eastern men must have been a pilot with crop-dusting experience. The other might have had experience handling a deadly biological weapon. All this was my speculation. Now, I said, we had to figure out what the next move by the terrorist would be. They had completed a practice run, but what was the use of a practice run if everyone who participated—except one—had died? We would only know by interrogating the person who killed the female pilot and then walked back into Mexico.

Rachel asked excitedly, "What if the third person did not walk back into Mexico? What if that person was the leader of the terrorist team in Southern California? What if he or she had hired the female pilot and needed to eliminate her when the terrorists had what they wanted from her? He or she could have been picked up at the Otay Mesa dump by someone who was harboring him or her in the area on the U.S. side of the border."

I said that I would make a few calls about the fingerprints. I contacted the Agency liaison with law enforcement in San Diego. She investigated the issue of the fingerprints, and she told me that five different persons' prints had been found in the car. The pilot's prints were most numerous. Some wiping of fingerprints had evidently been attempted, but a latent thumbprint of a known, formerly-convicted female drug runner named Belle Davis, age thirty-four, had been taken. She had been questioned by the police, and they reported that she had an iron-clad alibi for the time of the shooting of the pilot. She claimed that she had been sleeping that night with a deputy district attorney of the city, and he verified her statement asking only that the felon's statement not be reported in the press. The other three prints found in the car were from persons with no police records on the U.S. side of the border. Two of the prints matched prints taken from the corpses of two men found dead in the desert just north of the Mexican border. Rachel and I agreed that two possibilities existed to explain the facts. Either the female felon had lied or the person who left the unidentified print was our suspect.

"What are the chances that the pilot who flew me into Mexico knew the dead female pilot?" I made the call and my friend, the pilot, said that she knew the woman as a competent competitor, formerly Air Force Special Forces, who sometimes did jobs that she, herself would never take. For example, before she was killed, she had contracted to do a job for a female who had a questionable reputation. When she heard about the murder, my friend wondered whether that particular job had run afoul. I asked her what she knew about the female with the questionable rep, and she said that the woman, whose name was Belle something-or-another, was a convicted drug runner with a real attitude and interesting city connections. The woman had evidently approached my friend to perform the same mission, but on intuition, she had refused the contract even though the money was too good to be believed. Something just did not feel right about the deal at the time.

I told my friend to watch her six because the deal was much bigger than anyone supposed. It was a killing field, and I warned her to lie low for a while as things sorted out. She laughed and told me that she had seen it all. Packing a 45-caliber pistol that she knew how to use, she reiterated her desire to help me if she could, and we disconnected.

Rachel and I discussed what I had learned from my liaison contact and my pilot friend. She made a sidelong comment about all my muses, and I reminded her that she was the one I was talking with in a house we shared. Rachel thought that we had almost enough to make our move. She was still puzzled about the print for which we did not have a match. For now we put that issue on hold and focused on Belle Davis. Rachel suggested that it might be time to bring our friends the Blomfelds back into the picture. We had a long deliberation about this because we could play Belle Davis on either side of the field. If we guessed wrong, we would lose our game and possibly one of the Blomfelds. If we guessed right, we had to be ready to move to a conclusion fast.

It was time for lunch at the hamburger joint, and the Blomfelds were anxious to please. We gave them the entire picture, and we told them that we needed help sorting Belle Davis out. Would the Blomfelds take the approach for action?

I said, "The objective would be implemented interrogation, preferably on the Mexican side of the border. I do not like the connection to law enforcement and the prosecutor's office on this side. Who knows what kind of protection Belle Davis has, and from whom she has it?"

Rachel interposed, "I'm willing to help." After Mexico, she wanted to be part of the operation badly.

"It's better that you're out of this action, Rachel." I knew I was disappointing her, but everyone else nodded in agreement with my judgment. Rachel was not pleased. She pouted through the rest of our conversation.

Finally, when we began to make our list of questions for Belle Davis, Rachel came to life again from her pouting and withdrawal when turned down.

"No matter what you think, I'm going to help in any way I can." She chipped right in by grabbing a clipboard and making notes. In fact, she was very helpful in prioritizing our questions and making suggestions about alternative scenarios for the interrogation.

"Wouldn't someone like Belle Davis likely have protection on both sides of the border? Rosarita, therefore, might be a better venue than Tijuana." After this good suggestion, Rachel was on fire with others. She spoke with urgency and authority.

"It'll be essential to assure that Belle doesn't communicate with anyone from the moment of the snatch until she's been returned to the point of extraction or to a shallow grave."

On that cheery note, we discontinued our discussions and returned to our respective lairs.

Twenty-four hours later, the Blomfelds signaled that they were in the execution phase of our plan, and Rachel vanished. I did not know where Rachel had gone, but I knew that she was miffed that she was not included in the op. I was worried sick about her and quite upset. She had taken my Jag, and her Oshun blue dress and matching jewelry were gone from her closet. She had never left me without giving me an idea of where she was going. She was a free agent, I always maintained, but at this juncture in our mission, the dangers for all of us were becoming asymptotic. I feared that she might get caught in the crossfire, and I sincerely hoped that she had not decided to go to Rosarita to help the Blomfelds. I left a message on her cell phone that simply said, "Good luck. Be safe. XXX." I also signaled the Blomfelds that Rachel had gone clandestine to do I did not know what. Then I remained in the command center waiting for word from whoever would communicate with me. My company would normally have been Jack Daniels and Hiram Walker, but I decided on ice water with lime and aspirin because I might need to think clearly or swing into action depending on the circumstances. I began to recognize what Rachel had felt when I was on my op in Mexico. I had left her without an ability to connect to my operation on the assumption that I was protecting her. Now she felt disconnected and was off to do whatever she wanted because I had denied her the right to be on the mission. I did not regret my decision, but I did not like living with the unintended consequence.

Sometimes I hate it when I am right, and the Blomfelds proved me right about how to play Belle Davis. The Blomfelds led from the distaff side with Ruth, and, bingo, Belle was butch and tough. Belle fell for the female Blomfeld like a ton of bricks and the pair was off in a white chauffeured limo to Rosarita for lobsters roasted on the beach and a full box of little sex toys for an all-night debauch. The chauffeur, of course, was another Blomfeld, Ryan, who would discreetly serve as the muscle, although Belle said that she was perfectly safe south of the border because of her friends among the brass of the Federales. Belle was so confident of this that she agreed to turn off all her communications devices for the night to preserve their privacy. To prove it, she did so.

The Blomfelds reported that when they reached their rented beach house destination in Rosarita, the excited ladies immediately stripped naked and went to bed to play with their toys and each other. Belle Davis felt Ruth Blomfeld's hammerlock too late. Although Davis put up a valiant struggle, she was quickly overpowered by the two Blomfelds. Ruth got the needle in Belle's tattooed arm and pushed the plunger. She did not hesitate or have any regrets. This was not about lesbianism sodality, for Ruth it was about good and evil. The subsequent interrogation took two hours, all of which was ably recorded. I received the audio file at 3 a.m. with a detailed covering email. The Blomfelds promised to give me the X-rated video version after their return to the U.S. The essence of the interrogation, I discovered, was that a Deputy District Attorney of San Diego was Belle Davis's accomplice in a complex arrangement for criminal activities of all kinds. Numerous parties were evidently taking advantage of the porosity of the Mexican border and the corruptibility of officials on both sides of the border.

Belle had sung like a mockingbird about names, addresses, routes, conduits, bank accounts, networks, drugs—particularly the new heroin traffic, human trafficking, the Iranian connection, the terrorist leadership and their logistical support. Under the needle, Davis confessed to murdering the female pilot. She named the hitherto unknown owner of the fifth latent print from the pilot's car as the Iranian fixer and documented Quds Force terrorist, Abu Said. Davis gave her abductors the contact protocols for reaching Abu Said and, better, his current location and cell phone number.

The Blomfelds realized the value of the information that they had received, and they emailed that the priceless cache would please their Mossad masters very much. Belle Davis would never be prosecuted for all the crimes that she committed since her last conviction. The Blomfelds knew that they would be in danger if Belle told her protectors about the activities of this night. Belle Davis therefore would 'unfortunately' die of a drug overdose in the rented safe house. She would be found naked among her many sex toys in a sexually compromising position. Nothing would be discovered at the house pointing to the Blomfelds, who would wend their way back across the border in their white limo after an evening of fine dining south of the border.

At four a.m. I received the brief communication "K" from Rachel. I breathed a sigh of relief and wiped my brow, letting my shoulders relax for the first time in hours. I was glad that she was, for the moment, alive and okay. From her geoposition I reckoned that Rachel must be at the finest hotel in downtown San Diego. I took a chance and relayed her current position to the Blomfelds as they crossed the border.

The Blomfelds were dead tired from their exertions in Rosarita, but they were happy to serve as backup for Rachel if she had the need. They returned the limo to the rental agency and requested for it to be ready by noon after a thorough washing both inside and out. Complaining about how filthy the car had been with grime all over the inside, the siblings demanded that the renter use both towels and lotion on every inch of the interior. They said they would inspect the interior with white gloves and would either accept it or not based on their inspection.

The Blomfelds arrived at the hotel where Rachel was believed to be staying at dawn. They booked a room and texted, "RUOK? 324. 2Bs" to Rachel, who texted "K 533 TKS. BRUFUS 8 AM" back. That gave the Blomfelds time to take quick showers, check their arms and ammo and then position themselves discreetly in the hotel breakfast room before 8 a.m., when Rachel entered on the arm of the Deputy District Attorney of San Diego. Both had apparently had an athletic night together because of their skin tones and alertness. They had barely been seated and given their menus and coffee when the Deputy Distant Attorney received a call on his cell that caused him to turn very pale.

Stuttering and looking frantically all around the room, he excused himself from the table, saying that he was very sorry to go but it was lovely and he would be in touch. Without another word he bolted from the room in a panic.

Rachel took her date's frantic actions in stride. She called the waiter to her table and asked whether her meal could be billed to her hotel room. When she learned that it could be, she ordered the best breakfast on the menu and ate it with relish. After she ate, she went back to the Deputy District Attorney's room and packed her belongings. With slow movements showing that she was fully in charge of the situation, she left the hotel to recover my Jag. When she was on the road in the Jag, she texted the Blomfelds and me "K & Enroute Hburger Joint CU TKS!" She had completed her first clandestine meeting solo and was very proud of herself. I was proud of her too, but I was also afraid of the precedent she had set. Her freedom was liberation for her but sheer terror for me. We were going to have to discuss the new ground rules without diminishing her sense of achievement in taking initiative.

Rachel Wears a Veil

Rachel played with two cell phones at the dining room table in our safe house. One had been the property of the convicted felon Belle Davis, who had succumbed to a drug overdose administered by the Blomfeld siblings in Rosarita, Mexico. The other was her personal cell phone, which also served as a recorder and intelligence photo tool. She was very excited about what she was reviewing on her phone and almost spilled her coffee when she leaned over to show me one of the snaps of the Deputy District Attorney that she had made.

"I wouldn't have guessed that the Deputy Distant Attorney was uncircumcised and so small. He always came on like a macho man."

"Hahaha. That's rich, Rachel. The big man of San Diego is reduced to a caricature."

Our meeting with the Blomfelds at the hamburger joint had been a celebration of another successful mission. Intelligence sharing between the Mossad and the Agency had never been so open and candid. But then our working together was a secret kept closely held from both of our agencies. The official reaction to the Blomfelds' intelligence cache when Mossad Headquarters received it was a complete lockdown of the information and immediate debriefing in Jerusalem for both Blomfelds. The Institute knew nothing about my connection to the Rosarita op and neither did the Agency. Agency secrecy can work more than one way, fortunately.

So when I played the loyal employee and told that harridan Deputy Director of Operations about Abu Said's whereabouts in Mexico, she flew into a tirade that went on for over an hour with threats and recriminations sprinkled through screeching of the most blood-curdling kind. My telling her that the intelligence we harvested would get her a commendation and maybe set her up for a promotion to Director did nothing to calm her. She went at me again for going off the reservation and trying to change the subject. Didn't I know that I was breaking Company rules? And so forth.

Of course, my boss would never get my sources and methods from me and she knew it. She just liked to vent, and I could picture her flame-red hair sticking out on all sides of her head, her pointy stick fingers with nails colored with flame red OLI nail polish working on her cell phone, and her tiny feet in her flame-red flats doing a tap dance of indignation on the floor of her spacious seventh floor office at Langley Headquarters. Finally I told the Wicked Witch of the East that if she was not going to order a hit team to take out Abu Said using the existing Presidential Finding for his assassination, I would do so without her orders. Without wasting a second, I hung up to avoid the third eruption of Vesuvius.

Our call had been on speaker, so when it ended both Rachel and I laughed until we cried over my boss's incurable temper. I told Rachel that she would think for a while about the commendation and promotion, and then she would order an Agency hit as I had suggested. I just hoped that the hit would not be on me.

Rachel, rationalizing to calm me down while stroking my hand, said that she thought my boss would not likely take out the one agent who brought her all the crown jewels of intelligence about the threat. I gave her my 'you are sometimes so naïve' look, and Rachel got back to gleaning information from her phones. Her black hair glistened in the morning light, and her natural grace and motion made me happy that she was nearby.

We had verified, by implemented interrogation of Belle Davis, that the VEE cache we had been looking for was not in the LA area after all. Instead, it was being stored in a warehouse in Mexico for delivery through drug smuggling channels to Ocotillo, just as the exercise package had been delivered. We knew the precise location of the biological warfare package, and the Deputy Director of Operations had seen no problem with our infiltrating Mexico, stealing the package and bringing it to a secure biological warfare lab in the U.S. as soon as possible. We also knew exactly how many terrorists and drug smuggling goons were guarding the warehouse, which housed a large quantity of brown and white heroin as well as the VEE. My boss had not liked the idea of destroying the warehouse with the VEE inside. She did think that it would be fun to destroy it after the VEE had been safely extracted. We thought it would be exciting also. As for collateral damage, as long as only terrorists and drug smugglers died, she was okay with the op concept. Site intelligence indicated only one problem, which was the mosque and school that lay adjacent to the warehouse. She simply said that we should "deal with it."

After long deliberation, Rachel and I came up with a plan that surprised both of us. To execute our plan, we would need to enlist the help of Ruth Blomfeld, our old friend Dr. Marriott the vet and my female pilot friend Rosa

Sanchez. Our biggest headache was dealing with the possibility of collateral damage. Rachel studied the detailed aerial photograph of the site, and she came up with a workable solution. She and Ruth would go into the scene at night dressed head to toe in the same style burkas that the women of the terrorist community wore. They would carry weapons under their robes and make use of a diversionary fire to rush the women and children into a nearby building for safety's sake. Then they would join in the general melee. I said that extraction of the VEE canisters should occur at the same time as the diversionary fire because the terrorists would likely want to protect their biological warfare cache as a priority over everything else, their women and children included. In a sense, the diversionary fire was the best way for the terrorists to show us exactly where the VEE canisters were in that warehouse. We did not have a plan for the contingency that the VEE was released into the air somehow, but we thought it was better to have the VEE released where it now was rather than offshore near LA. I wanted Rachel to be upwind of the VEE in any case. The biological substance was nearly one hundred percent lethal, after all.

When we ran the plan by Ruth, the experienced Mossad agent asked what would happen if the terrorist women were armed and resisted. My look told her to draw her own conclusion. When we ran the plan by Dr. Marriott, the vet gave detailed instructions on what the canisters looked like and on safe procedures for handling and loading them. He also said he would be standing by upon our return with an emergency biological weapons response team to take custody of the VEE canisters. I told the pilot that she needed to stay by the escape aircraft and to be sure that it was properly refueled and ready to take off when things got hot. I also gave her our priorities. Our first priority was for her to transport the VEE canisters back to the Biological Warfare Team at the airport. I told her to work with Dr. Marriott to fashion cradles for the VEE canisters since she would not want them to roll around in flight. Even if no passengers could fit in the plane once the canisters had been loaded, her concern was the canisters, not the passengers.

Finally, when Ryan Blomfeld returned from Jerusalem, I told him about his role as the driver of our ground transportation, a Jeep. If anything happened to the aircraft or the pilot prior to takeoff, Ryan was to drive the VEE canisters into the desert and to unload and bury them where we could find them later.

As part of our preparations, I took Rachel for weapons familiarization and discovered that she was a natural marksman. She knew how to stand, kneel and lie down with rifle or pistol and how to put her safety on and take it off. Able to group five rounds within the area of a quarter at twenty-five paces, the woman had clearly handled weapons before, and she relished them. She knew about hang fires and ejection jams and how to field strip her weapons in the dark. She knew so much about these technical matters that I was reminded how little I knew about her past, and I became suspicious of how she had acquired her skills. Instead of confronting her about my suspicions, I told her that she would make a great terrorist, and she took a pose that should have made the cover of Time magazine. We practiced covering fire, withdrawal under fire and invasive advance under fire. She said that I must have watched a lot of western movies. Then it was my turn to pose like John Wayne, and we laughed.

The whole team assembled at the airport to drill the scenario. It was a good thing that we did so because Rosa Sanchez's vintage Cessna 172 Skyhawk aircraft could accommodate only four passengers without the precious cargo and only two passengers including the pilot with a full load of canisters. I had fortunately factored this into the plan. Ryan would drive Ruth and me in the Jeep to and from our objective in Mexico. Rosa and Rachel would ride in and out aboard the aircraft, which would ferry our weapons, ammo and burkas. Rosa briefed Rachel on airborne procedures. She then took Rachel for a test run and let her take over steering in case she should need to help in the event that Rosa was wounded in action.

With the ground crew, I briefed our plan and contingencies for the assault and extraction phases. The Blomfelds, Rachel, and I walked into the desert to fire a few practice rounds advancing and retreating. Ruth was pleasantly surprised by Rachel's excellent marksmanship. Seeing how Rachel knew how to handle a gun, she moved to the next matter, the burkas. Ruth had been shopping for burkas, so she and Rachel tried on their disguises. Ruth taught Rachel how to walk slowly in her burka and how not to stumble over her long, flowing black garment by using her hands to lift the cloth. During the operation, Ruth was to do all the talking because she was fluent in Farsi and Arabic. Rachel could ululate but otherwise remain silent. Rachel practiced ululating, and everyone, including her, laughed.

We confirmed how we would communicate before, during, and after the assault. I showed Rosa where the Biological Warfare Team would position themselves to wait for her returning flight. I counted out twenty-thousand dollars for Rosa to cover half of her pay for the job. The other half of her remuneration would be paid on successful completion of the mission. Satisfied that we were now as ready as we ever would be, we confirmed the dates and times for the departure of the Jeep and the plane and we retreated to our separate lairs.

This trip to Mexico was emotionally complicated because Rachel would be accompanying me on this mission, and things were going to get really intense. We would have to do some shooting, and our targets would be shooting back. Casualties were likely. *What would I do if Rachel should be wounded or even killed in action?* I was nearly beside myself with concern. Rachel knew what was going through my mind, and she did her best to console me without going overboard and getting mawkish. Making love the night before my departure, Rachel took the top position straddling me, and as she leaned down to kiss me and her hair fell on my face, I felt a hot tear hit my cheek.

We met the Blomfelds at the hamburger joint for an early breakfast and for my shift from the Jag to the Jeep. We waved goodbye to Rachel, who would depart in two days for the aircraft ride with Rosa. Our drive to Mexico was uneventful and even pleasant. We stayed in a seedy motel nearby our objective and scouted the small airfield where the Cessna airplane would land the next day. The airport was unattended, but anything might happen in this drug running haven, so we prepared to subdue any of the opposition who might show up at our party.

The infiltration went like clockwork. Rosa and Rachel arrived right on time at the airfield in the late afternoon. The Blomfelds and I unloaded the plane and transferred our things to the Jeep. Ruth and Rachel dressed in their burkas and rode in the back of the Jeep to the edge of the sleepy village where the warehouse lay. We arrived as the sun set, and Ryan and I took positions on either side of the warehouse. Ryan had a scoped rifle, and he went to the roof of a building across from the warehouse. I stayed at ground level in the shadows by the mosque. Ruth and Rachel ambled very slowly down the street that ran through the town, and both ran past the mosque on the left and the warehouse on the right.

From my hiding place, I counted five of the opposition in the street outside the warehouse. Two were seated and three were walking about and talking in Farsi with each other. The mosque and school looked empty, but then we heard the sound of a muezzin calling the holy to worship.

The street came alive with Moslems going to the mosque for worship. Ruth and Rachel vanished into the shadows along the street. I watched as the throng gathered and entered the mosque, the men through one door, and the women in burkas through the other. Worship took about thirty minutes, and then the worshippers went back to where they had come from. The same five men returned to their positions as guards of the warehouse. The women went to what was apparently a communal hotel dwelling down the street from the warehouse, in the direction where Ruth and Rachel had disappeared.

I signaled Ryan to be ready, and we both took aim. At that moment I heard screams and saw movement down by the hotel. The guards became animated and looked around to see what was happening. Ryan's shots rang out. I began to advance on the warehouse, holding fire until I was close enough to make sure kills. I was within fifteen feet of my first victim before I fired. My target crumpled and dropped to the street. I counted two other terrorists down. That meant two had retreated inside the warehouse.

The din by the hotel was now very clamorous. Ululations and cries filled the air. Three figures in burkas came running down the street towards the warehouse. The figure in the lead fired a shot towards where Ryan was positioned. She was shot dead by one of the two burka-clad figures who were following her. From their hand motions, it was clear to me that Ruth and Rachel were taking positions on either side of the street to prevent any of the women terrorists from interfering with our op.

Ryan descended from the roof and reemerged opposite the warehouse into which I was advancing fast and low. He came right in behind me. After we had entered, we kept away from the door because with the light differential we could be easy targets. The two terrorists were where we expected them to be, not by the large bales of drugs on the left but by the canisters that lay in a gated enclosure on the right. The terrorists had taken refuge in a cage, so they were sitting ducks. Ryan shot the terrorist on the left, and I shot the one on the right as he aimed to fire at the flash of Ryan's rifle.

We turned on our torches and checked the rest of the warehouse. We had ten minutes to do what was needed. I told Ryan to get the Jeep, and while he was bringing our transport, I readied the VEE canisters for transport. There were five canisters of exactly the dimensions that the good vet had described. That was one fewer canister than we had figured on, but then one had been used in the experiment at Ocotillo. That was just as well because I was now confident that the cargo would fit in the airplane without a problem. Ryan backed the Jeep into the warehouse, and we both lifted and positioned the canisters in the Jeep. I rigged the explosives that we had brought in the Jeep from the plane so that they would detonate when I pressed a remote control button. We then drove carefully out of the warehouse and into the street.

Up to that point our op had been flawless in both planning and execution. I was waiting for Mr. Murphy and his famous laws to show up, and I was not surprised when they appeared in the form of five burka-clad terrorists rushing us from the area of the hotel down the street. Leading them was the imam who had conducted their worship only minutes ago. I raised my pistol and Ryan raised his rifle, and when we fired, we heard many other reports of weapons including Uzis. The gun battle had begun in earnest. I do not believe in retreating once I have committed to an action, as that shows lack of resolve and good planning, so I motioned to Ryan to move right towards the advancing attackers, slowly. As he drove I continued to fire. I noticed that much of the firing was coming from either side of the street ahead, but it was not directed at us. Ruth and Rachel had a turkey shoot. Ryan had killed the imam with his rifle in our fusillade. I had taken out one of the five female terrorists. Ruth took out two others, and Rachel took out the other two. Ryan now turned on his headlights, first dim and then bright. As we weaved in and out around the bodies in the street, our ladies threw off their confining burkas and jumped aboard the moving vehicle. We passed the hotel, and three other burka-clad figures were in the doorway. The women did not hesitate to cut them down in a heap, their weapons clattering as they fell. As we left the town I pressed the detonator button, and the warehouse exploded and burst into flames that lighted the field of carnage like a carnival. The women watched our rear as the Jeep proceeded deliberately to our airport destination.

Mr. Murphy was not finished for the evening. Ahead at the airport we heard an exchange of gunfire. Ryan slowed so that Ruth, Rachel and I could dismount and run ahead. We saw that Rosa had gotten away from her plane and was now under fire from three shooters who had just landed at the airport to pick up a load of drugs. Their drugs were, of course, going up in flames from our explosion, so the druggies were furious and taking their frustration out on the nearest target, who was Rosa. I was glad of three things. First, they were lousy shots. Second, when they fired they exposed their own positions. Third, they never saw us coming. Almost simultaneously we three fired at each of the three targets, and we hit our marks. The firefight was over. I raced to Rosa to see that she was all right, and she said that she was. I asked Rosa whether she could be ready to fly when we got the VEE canisters loaded. She nodded. We all got busy with Ruth, Rosa, and Rachel guarding and Ryan and I loading, and, once again, our plan was on track.

Few things are more gratifying to me than accomplishing two missions for the price of one. The roaring fire at the warehouse symbolized what I thought should happen to all drug caches in the world. The transport of weapons of mass destruction out of the hands of terrorists and into the hands of our proper authorities was an Agency dream come true.

We still had our evacuation to handle, but our chances began to look good. Assured that the payload was secure and all our remaining arms and ammo except for three loaded handguns and my remaining explosives were well stowed, Rosa and Rachel climbed aboard the aircraft, taxied and took off. Ryan and I rigged explosives on the drug-running plane while Rosa took cell phone pictures of each of the druggies whom we had killed for our albums.

We then climbed aboard the Jeep and drove the first leg of our trip back north. Before arriving at our motel, we decided to offload and bury two handguns in the desert. Ruth kept her handgun ready for action and safely tucked it down her trousers. That night I received a text from Rachel, simply "K" and I knew that now the Biological Warfare Team was conveying the VEE canisters from the plane to their land vehicle. The mission had been completed except for our homecoming. I remained on guard just in case, but our trip back to the border was uneventful. Exhilarated, we returned to LA via Interstate 5 and met Rachel at the hamburger joint for a hot wash-up.

The most surprising thing about this mission was a brief text from my harridan boss. She texted "BZ, AH. FYI Abu Said Down. L, DDO!" and it included her avatar, which was a red-haired, wild-eyed stick-form bitch throwing a tantrum. Rachel laughed when she saw the Deputy Director of Operations' avatar. I said it hardly did the harridan justice because the real thing looked far worse than her avatar. I held the avatar next to Rachel's face and was about to say something about her resemblance when Rachel pummeled me with her fists and said, "Oh, you!"

We laughed, and then I ran to get in my swimming suit. Rachel was racing me to get hers on, and we tied. Actually neither of us got our suit on, but we were so close to doing so. We had stopped for a long kiss, and then, well, she melted into my arms and I grew strong and long and hard. It was hours later that we took our third shower together and dried each other off.

"I'm very glad you survived our mission. I can hardly believe how much you've learned since we met and how very proud of you I am." Rachel blushed all over her beautiful body and came over to sit in my naked lap. She squirmed a little as if to settle down, and she put her head on my shoulder. One long, small arm reached around my back and one small hand gently rubbed my chest and stomach hairs.

She looked deep into my eyes, and then she whispered in my ear, "I am soooo hungry." Even after all we had been through together, so was I.

- 164 -

Rachel and the Law

The Blomfelds did not gain much from our latest escapade in Mexico. I suppose that Rachel and I, as well as the Agency, owed them and the Mossad a big favor for what they had done for us. I could not have accomplished the weapons of mass destruction mission without them. Seizing enough biological weapons to have killed the entire population of Greater LA was not something you did every day or even once in a very long career. We had pulled off this miracle largely due to the intelligence that the Blomfelds had gained beforehand, with their implemented interrogation of the convicted felon Belle Davis and their operational support during the mission itself.

All of our work had been done outside either CIA's or Mossad's sanctions as rogue operations planned and executed by Ruth and Ryan Blomfeld and Rachel and I. The Blomfelds had been our partners far beyond the boundaries of a single mission, and as planners and operators they were our accomplices and friends. In the course of our collaboration, we had together inadvertently stumbled on information implying strong connections between many criminal activities in Southern California and international espionage networks.

Most notably we discovered the links between the criminal activities of drug running and human trafficking and the Islamic terrorist network throughout Mexico,

Central America and South America. When the Islamic network infiltrated weapons of mass destruction into the U.S. through our porous southern border, the clear and present danger of the network of mosques and religious schools became glaringly evident. For my money, the entire network of interlocking factions should have been dismantled and destroyed. The Blomfelds agreed with me and so, I thought, did the Mossad.

Anyway, Rachel held the key to pursuing the Southern California criminal connections. The key lay in the most unlikely source—the Deputy District Attorney of San Diego. Having lost his key criminal operator, the deceased felon Belle Davis, the Deputy District Attorney was left clueless how to proceed, except that he had just spent one of the most enjoyable evenings of his life in the company of beautiful Rachel. Information that Rachel had purloined from the Deputy District Attorney implied that by mining him and his accomplices, the criminal underworld of San Diego would become apparent. That alone would not be interesting to the Agency because criminal activity was the domain of law enforcement. Because of the interplay of the criminals and the spies in San Diego and Tijuana, however, the Agency could take an interest. Such an interest would have to be oblique so that Agency ops did not run afoul of law enforcement ops and vice versa. The penchant for secrecy on both sides rendered anyone who got in the middle an easy target. So I was going to have to let Rachel run with her adventures separately from mine, or I was going to have to embrace her operations as my own. She knew that the Blomfelds had provided backup for her at the hotel where she had slept with the Deputy District Attorney. She knew that she might have needed their help, although that was not necessary on her first exposure.

So I accepted Rachel's play as a part of my own larger agenda. Her intuition, I had learned, was at least as good as my own. She could perform what I think of as intuitive integration on the fly, and that is what differentiates a great agent from an also-ran. Rachel was a survivor who figured the angles in real time as she operated. She was not a victim of the Agency planning syndrome. Instead, she was agile and adaptive. She could take the initiative and follow through. I had told her that I was proud of her after our last foray into Mexico. Rachel had performed well on her own. Besides, I marveled at her independence. I was beginning to trust her judgment. She was my lover and my protégé, but she had increasingly become my colleague and my partner too. There with her spoon playing in her yogurt and her constant cup of hot coffee standing by, she was my muse and my sphinx.

"Anderson," she said, "The Deputy District Attorney called again and asked me to join him at the hotel on Thursday. He called it 'our usual room.' What do you think?"

I thought that I should go along and break the man's scrawny neck or work over his smiling, handsome face until it was pure pulp, or punch his kidneys until he screamed for his Mommy. But since I am civilized, long-suffering and patient, I tried to calm down before I responded.

"Would you like to double date with the Blomfelds?"

She considered this carefully and her eyes squinted in concentration. Then she said that she would handle this matter alone. It was important that she not allow the Deputy District Attorney to make any connection between their love nest and all the operations that were destroying the man's criminal empire.

"What if," she asked, "the Deputy District Attorney began to wonder whether I was planted to divert him while his former lover was being questioned and killed in Rosarita? What would you rate my chances of survival after he discovered that I had done exactly that?" She was making my point, so I let her fly freely. I did not lose interest. I just lost control. This way Rachel was teaching me to let her become self-sufficient, but it hurt me to let her have things her way when she might be tortured or killed, or both in our common battle against evil. I rationalized that the war we were always in required sacrifices. Still, I did not want to sacrifice Rachel through any insouciance on my part.

Early Thursday afternoon, Rachel donned her armor of the Oshun blue dress and matching jewelry. With her hair in black ringlets and her fingernails and toenails done in Oshun blue, she looked like a fashion model fresh off the runway, and I told her so as I waved goodbye. I said that I would look for her texts if she got the chance. She smiled and waved as she sped away in my Jag. My stomach knotted in worry the moment she drove out of sight.

Spying requires a lot of waiting, whether you are the agent lurking on the pavement or the agent waiting in a secret room for the report from some other agent who stood in harm's way. While I waited, I continued combing through my notes for any loose end that we had not considered. From the sources we had used, we had gleaned intelligence that allowed us to interdict weapons of mass destruction operations at seven major U.S. ports and one staging outpost in Mexico. Any single one of those weapons of mass destructions operations could have caused panic greater than occurred on September 11, 2001.

I reasoned that the threat could regroup in a heartbeat and that other weapons of mass destruction materials might now be stored near other ports and major cities. Perhaps other terrorist networks were involved than those that we had discovered during our missions.

My imagination was on fire trying to game like the enemy. I knew I was not alone in doing this, but I always did have the ability to think 'out of the box.' My colleagues usually relied only on what they knew or what they had been told. My kind of blue-sky thinking was anathema to them. Among Agency folks, I had always been the grateful pariah agent in their midst. Some called me the turd in the punch bowl. I was always underappreciated for my hard work and patriotism. It comes with the territory for rogues like me. I'd rather have my freedom without all the bullshit. Go figure.

I decided to meet the Blomfelds at the hamburger joint just to clear the air and lay down where our intelligence gaps now were. I told them that Rachel was on a side mission and would not be coming. At the meeting I patiently retraced everything we had discovered, and then I told Ruth and Ryan that I was wracking my brain over other possible scenarios that we might have overlooked while we were passionately pursuing our leads.

The Blomfelds were glad to know my status. They had not yet taken the opportunity to tell me about Ryan's visit to Mossad Headquarters in Jerusalem. I remembered that Ryan had been recalled to Mossad Headquarters shortly after our last adventure in Mexico. Ryan said that during that visit his masters had been very pleased with the intelligence that both of the Blomfelds had unearthed in Southern California. Their analysts were now hard at work integrating that information with global intelligence and information that they had gathered from many other sources.

"The Mossad never sleeps," Ryan said, "any more than the CIA sleeps. The Mossad is considering transferring both Ruth and me to other venues around the world. Such is the reward for being productive where they happened to be entrenched. I expect both my sister and I to receive transfers within six months." I was devastated by this news.

"We are both sad to have to break up our team."

"I'm very sorry to learn about your impending transfers. The same kind of transfer might also happen to me, but I am such a pariah that many are happy to have me bottled up in a backwater instead of playing on the great stage of the world. We rogues are not automatons. We have feelings." Right then I felt that I wanted to break a lot of china and out-roar the sea. I could do nothing to keep our team together, but that did not mean I would like the situation. Bureaucrats in Israel unwittingly pulled my team apart because they were insensitive morons.

Ruth said, "Because Israel's enemies are everywhere, Mossad has to be everywhere also. The well-publicized bombings in Argentina and Bulgaria reminded the Mossad that Jews everywhere are at risk daily."

I had to agree with her.

"Has it not been true," Ruth asked, "that in the U.S. Islamists have plotted against rabbis, Jewish schools, and Jewish institutions? Some in Israel saw even the explosive events of September 11, 2001, as an expression of hatred toward the wealthy Jews who owned the World Trade Center."

I retorted, "The U.S. is, like Israel, both a location and an idea. A Jew and an American have a common distinction from the rest of the world's inhabitants—yet they hold unusual ideas, like family and freedom, that are antithetical to each other."

Ryan nodded sagely in agreement. Ruth was not convinced.

She asked, "When had Americans suffered a Holocaust?"

I answered, "Many Americans are Jewish survivors of the Holocaust."

I let that thought settle. Then I segued to the current situation. I stated, "Rachel is following her own trail in San Diego. She is now with the Deputy District Attorney, the same man with whom she slept when you served as her backup protection."

Ruth seemed alarmed to hear this. She and Rachel were close, and I could see that she was doing the mental calculus about Rachel's desire to pursue this particular source.

She asked me, "How long has it been since you last had word from Rachel?"

"It's been forty-eight hours since she had last texted me 'K' and at that time she was in the same geolocation as before—the hotel."

Ruth said distantly that she and Ryan had to be going now. Her thoughts seemed to be somewhere else. So she hustled Ryan out of the restaurant and drove him away into the golden California sunshine. I returned to the safe house, somewhat unsettled by what Ruth's instincts had told her.

By 6 p.m. I had still not received a text update from Rachel. I did see the Deputy District Attorney appear on national television news discussing his plans for eradicating crime from Southern California. I thought that the man's hypocrisy was patent. He was apparently looking for a rung up the political ladder with his impassioned talk about crime and criminals. When he arrived at his peroration, I began to become alarmed because the Deputy District Attorney's answer for the crime was lots of money—Arab money. He said that with seed funding from Saudi Arabia and Qatar, he could create the strongest IT for law enforcement in the world. He smiled with his pearly teeth and waved with his milk-white, perfectly manicured hand. I used the channel changer and wondered whether I should take a bath to wash the scum that he had figuratively put all over me with his talk about Arab money.

When I pondered the Deputy District Attorney's comment further, I wondered why he had focused his talk on the beneficence of Sunni nations instead of the Shiite nation of Iran. His known criminal connections were to the Iranians, and they were Shiites, not Sunnis. Was the Deputy District Attorney trying to deflect the public's attention from his Shiite connections? Why would he do that? The September 11, 2001 terrorists had predominantly been Sunnis from Saudi Arabia. More than a few of the suicidal terrorists who commandeered the jetliners on the fatal day of the cataclysmic atrocity were known to have resided near San Diego in the two years prior to their hijackings. I reasoned that I would have to ask Rachel what was going on in the head of the Deputy District Attorney. After her latest contact with him, she might have some inkling about his thought process vis-à-vis the Saudis.

At a few minutes before midnight I received an urgent text message from Ruth Blomfeld that Rachel was in trouble. I was immediately on full alert, anxious to find out what was going on. Ruth texted that she knew where Rachel was—the hotel, but Ruth could not help because she was Jewish and also Mossad-connected. Ruth asked me to drive as fast as legally possible to meet her at the hotel where the Deputy District Attorney conducted his nightly trysts. Traffic was light, and I drove fast down Interstate 5 to San Diego. I parked on the street outside the hotel and bounded up the steps to meet Ruth and Ryan.

Ruth grabbed me by the arm and said, "Rachel is being held hostage in the suite that the Deputy District Attorney habitually uses for his affairs. She's being restrained by three or four Arab men."

Ryan continued, "Two of the Arabs seem to be refined civilians, but they are actually ruthless Saudi intelligence officers whom we know from working in the Middle East. On the surface Rachel's constraint looks like protection, but the Arab agents are definitely holding her in the room by force and keeping the Deputy District Attorney out of the room for some reason unknown to us."

Ruth, beside herself with worry for Rachel's safety, explained, "The Deputy District Attorney approached the door of the room and asked to be allowed inside. He was told to go away and do only what he is told to do. If Ryan or I do anything to free Rachel, the incident would be perceived in the press as a provocative Israeli action against Arabs on American soil."

She continued, "Rachel is not Jewish or Israeli, so she would be considered an ordinary civilian for whom Israel would have no binding interest."

I understood what Ruth was telling me.

"Will you let me have your gun with the silencer?"

She nodded, screwed the silencer on the gun barrel and gave it to me. I then went with the gun stashed in my pants into the hotel. I walked right past the empty desk straight back to the empty kitchen area.

I was on autopilot, my sole concern being to find Rachel and get her out of this hotel alive. Becoming the total operator now, I thrust all my emotions into the inner recesses of my mind. I didn't know what I was going to do until I did it. Finding a waiter's jacket on a hook, I put it on and commandeered a pushcart on wheels. The pushcart held a covered meal with a wine bucket and bottle of wine on the side rack. I found and added to the service a small vase with a rose and grabbed several white cloth napkins. Slicking back my hair with both my hands, I took a deep breath and moved to the elevator. I removed the gun with the silencer and put it under the pile of napkins on the top of the service. I then pressed the button for the fifth floor.

When I arrived at the Deputy District Attorney's love pad, I knocked softly on the door and waited for the door to open. The door cracked open a little, two eyes surveyed me, and then an Arab opened the door wide and gestured for me to roll the food inside. When I entered the main living space, I saw two men seated on either side of what must have been the main suite with its double doors closed. The men were clearly thugs who had been told to sit and wait until they were told to do something else.

The man who had asked me inside was interested in what I had brought in the covered dish, and he was about to lift it when I shot him between the eyes and then shot the man to the left of the double-door to the suite and the man to the right of it. Thinking only of my objective, I had no feelings whatsoever about eliminating the scum. Taking a deep breath before proceeding and being energized by fear for Rachel and mounting rage against her captors, I marched to the double-doors of the suite and kicked them open.

There trying to force himself on Rachel was a fourth Arab man, with his pants down and his ugly penis fully erect and uncircumcised. In his right hand he was brandishing a long, bright sword and in his left hand he held his distended, erect penis. He had pulled up Rachel's dress and she was holding it under duress. Apparently, he had just torn down her undies, which lay around her ankles. He did nothing more than that, except drop his sword as he fell. A trickle of blood glistened from a small hole in his forehead, marking where I had executed the man. I looked Rachel in the eyes and asked her whether she was injured. She was shaking on the verge of tears and shook her head quickly to the left then the right, looking down in shame. I told her gently but firmly to pull up her drawers and then pull down and straighten her dress. When she had finished, I took her hand and walked her swiftly through the corpses in the front room to the front door.

From the front door I looked out both ways down the hallway. Seeing no one coming from either direction, I took Rachel quickly to the elevator and pressed the down arrow. We entered the elevator after the bell rang, and we calmly descended to the ground floor in silence. Fortunately no one else was using the elevator. My mission was now to get Rachel clear, so I resisted any resort to sentiment. When we emerged from the elevator, I placed Rachel's arm over mine. We departed the hotel with confidence as if we were a loving couple going to a nightclub or a late-night movie, perhaps both. What could be more natural? I asked Rachel where she had parked the Jag, and she gestured in the right direction.

As we walked to the Jag, I picked up my cell and told Ryan he should drive my Jeep to LA and meet us at the hamburger joint with it in the morning. I said that Ruth should meet us there also. Once we reached the Jag, Rachel got in the passenger side and I drove. I drove just above the speed limit, but not so fast that we attracted attention. Behind, I saw two cars pull up to align with mine.

I looked straight ahead into the black California night. Rachel was looking out the window, through the nothingness that extended all the way to our destination in LA.

"It's going to be all right. Try to relax. You're okay. You're with me."

Rachel nodded slightly, indicating that she heard what I was saying. I continued as much for me as for her. We both had to come down from our very different adrenaline surges.

"Ruth and Ryan are right behind us. Those sirens that you hear in the distance are not for us. They are heading for the godforsaken city that we just left."

I held out my hand, palm up, and after a time she took it. She raised my hand to her mouth and held it there against her lips, sobbing quietly. She held it all the way back to Los Angeles as I drove through the desert. The dawn was just breaking as we pulled into the hamburger joint for our meeting with the Blomfelds.

We four sat on the steps of the hamburger joint until it opened for breakfast. Rachel had hugged each of us in turn for coming to the rescue. She had difficulty talking at first. I had to encourage her by being steady and reassuring. When she had calmed down, she took a deep breath and gave us a blow by blow account of her time in the Deputy District Attorney's love nest.

When she was done, we had a whole new perspective on what was happening in the Southern

California criminal world. Although Rachel had been through a harrowing experience, she had come home with the hard evidence we needed to make headway. I was thankful that Ruth had taken the initiative to discover what was happening after I did not get a text from Rachel for forty-eight hours. What if she had not done so? I was glad that was no longer a possibility, but I had been given the scare of a lifetime. By raising the alarm, I was stimulated to take immediate action, and I found that there was no way the Blomfeld's could take the necessary measures to free Rachel from her Arab captors.

To our surprise, not only Rachel but the Deputy District Attorney had been held captive. The reason that he had gone on international news channels to embrace the Sunni funding offer was that the Saudi intelligence operatives had threatened to kill Rachel in his love nest if he did not. Of course, the Deputy District Attorney did not care one way or another about Rachel's life. He did care about scandal that could be associated with him. Rachel was a liability if she should be killed in a location that was associated with him. Additionally, the Deputy District Attorney desperately needed an international ally at a time when his links with the Iranian terrorists had ceased to exist because of our operations against them.

We figured that the Deputy District Attorney might have a tough time disassociating himself from the quintuple murders that had taken place in his suite at the hotel, but nothing ever appeared in the papers about the mess I had left in that suite. Rachel was never identified as a person of interest. In the clean up and cover up after the event, it was as if five Muslim men had gone directly to Heaven by divine intervention.

The Deputy District Attorney had no reason to look for murderers. He might have had reason to look for Rachel, but he never called her cell phone number again. He had evidently erased the entire nightmarish incident from his malleable brain. He never again went on international television touting an Arab-funded solution to the problems of crime and justice in San Diego. All these perspectives came out gradually over the next three weeks. At the time of our hot wash-up meeting at the hamburger joint, we only knew that Rachel was now safe and uninjured. Ruth suggested that she have a medical exam, just in case, and we arranged for that to happen later—again, all was clear.

What both intrigued and illuminated the Blomfelds was the shift in the center of geopolitical gravity from the Shiite involvement to the Sunni involvement. Mossad was, Ryan told us, more interested in a Shiite play because of Iran and Hezbollah. He said that a Hamas involvement would be a more local and regional Israeli issue, but it did not have the importance of anything with an Iranian connection. At the highest levels the CIA might have the same view, but I neither confirmed nor denied his allegation. I did say that, once again, Rachel and I were in their debt. I felt honored and eternally grateful for what they had done. I was not surprised by their loyalty, which was part of their character.

I told them that I fully understood why they had been unable to take action at the hotel, and I would appreciate their not elucidating what happened there to anyone, particularly Mossad, about what I may or may not have done. Ryan said that he personally had no knowledge of anything that happened at the hotel. He and his sister had driven to San Diego to see the sights and returned to LA afterwards, period. Ruth said the same. I laughed and joked that it was good that we did not meet at the hamburger joint this morning for breakfast or taste this wonderful coffee in such good company. We all broke and returned to our separate digs. I have no idea what the Blomfelds did, but Rachel and I went straight to bed and did not awaken until late afternoon. Then we went down to the beach hand in hand for a long walk on the drying line in silence to watch the sun go down over the vast Pacific.

Rachel and the Harridan

Rachel had not been harmed during her stay in San Diego, although it was a close call. I let her come to grips with what she had experienced pretty much on her own. I was there for her if she felt she needed to talk, but she needed to take what happened deep within her psyche and come to grips with it. I could not go there with her. I had no idea what ghosts resided in all the caverns of her mind. What happens to any person when the creepy nightmares that they laugh at in the morning light become real hideous creatures with long swords that strip and threaten to kill while they rape and despoil? I was for a time driven by chthonic feelings that raged for some form of apocalyptic revenge against Islamism or even the whole Arab race. Rachel brought me back from the brink of madness when she told me it did not matter since I had found her when she needed me most, and I had done the only thing that could be done under the circumstances.

"I felt so helpless against those monsters. There seemed to be no way out. Then you appeared. Oh, Anderson, I am so very thankful. The worst is over now. I'm safe. Don't hate beyond the boundaries of the situation. We have too much focused work to do to become derailed by scum. If we are derailed by such monsters, then the monsters win."

As if taking her cue from the word 'monsters' the harridan Deputy Director of Operations called me on her cell to launch into one of her tirades. This time she was harping about my vouchers. One I had failed to sign properly. Another did not have the proper receipts. A third was going to be denied entirely unless I resubmitted with a different rationale. On and on she railed about my vouchers. Then she began railing about sharing data. She was frantic because Mossad had called the Director congratulating him on collaborating on critical ventures that he knew nothing about. The Prime Minister himself was going to praise the Agency to the President of the United States for services rendered above and beyond anything that Israel expected. My boss was furious because she knew nothing about the critical ventures but she suspected that I, Anderson, had been at work behind the scenes.

I pleaded ignorance and innocence to all charges. I was not the man, I did not suffer, I was not there. I pleaded guilty to whatever sins I had actually committed, but where is the sin to be owned as mine? I told my boss that I had been focusing on the problem of weapons of mass destruction being used against the U.S. I said that she knew that was true. She herself had done heroic work in that line, far more than I ever could do at my lowly level in the organization. I groveled and shrank my role to carrying out the Agency trash and poking in the international weeds on both sides of the border. I praised the Deputy Director of Operations and the Director to the skies. What could I do that they did not enable by their authorization, funding and support? Rachel heard all this on the speaker phone, and she could hardly contain herself from laughing outright and rolling on the floor.

Only when my boss got to her punch line, did I feel it like a body blow. The harridan laughed herself, not one of her halting cackles or her ironical sneering chortles, but a belly laugh coming from deep within her somewhere the sun never shines.

She said simply, "When I send you the very best we have and you almost get her killed, I just don't think I understand you anymore. Think about what you are doing. And if you so much as endanger one black hair on her head, I will have you terminated with extreme prejudice, you vile bastard. If she is listening, and I am sure she is, let her know that I am glad she is still alive. You would be nothing without her, nada, nil, zilch! Put that in your corncob pipe, mister, and smoke it till you are raw! Oh, yes, and have a nice day, you two. We have lots of work to do. Ta ta!"

I wished to God I had not heard those words. I stared at Rachel with a searching look that begged her to deny it. She was trying to look very small indeed, and so contrite you would have thought me an ogre or worse. Sir Galahad I was figured just a few moments ago. Or St. George saving the maiden chained to the rock from the marauding dragon from the sea. Now I was faced with a reality that I had glimpsed but tried to deny. Rachel was not Rachel. I had taken a viper in my nest. Rachel was worse than a viper, she was a mole. She had done what? I needed air and space.

I stuttered, "Excuse me, I'm going out to get some air on the beach." Rachel said nothing. She did not try to stop me. And then I walked right out of the safe house, right down to the vast Pacific rising beyond the horizon, and I continued into the waves to my waist, then my chest and I was suddenly swimming toward East Asia with bold strokes, my shoes cloying and my clothes sticking to me. I swam and swam, the cold water feasting on my warmth, my energy boiling over as the rage passed through me again and again. Bested by my harridan Deputy Director of Operations. *Deceived by my angel Rachel, my own creation, my daughter, my mentee, my protégé, my what? My concubine? No. My love? Why, yes! Perfidious. Changeling. Snipe. Traitor. Fraud!* I was treading water as I saw a flashing form swim under and around me, and then pop up in front of me with a mermaid's head and a roseate body.

It was Rachel, and she was naked as the day she was born, swimming like an otter in this frigid water, trying to tell me by her movements that it was all right, after all. She was attempting to make amends. I should have been angry and ignored her. Through my mind went many conflicting thoughts, but I could not hate this woman if I tried. She had become an essential part of me. I was the fool, not she. Her sudden appearance looking so vulnerable and desirable broke the ice that had temporarily formed around my heart.

When Rachel finally came right up to me face to face, I took her in my arms and squeezed her. I realized that she was shivering, and I motioned that we should strike for shore at once lest she should freeze to death. I tore off my shoes and my clothing as rapidly as I could so that we could make good speed. And then we swam together like seals slipping through the swells, turning over and over in the salty sea, emerging on the surf line and striding through the crunching waves to the shore where we fell on our knees in the gritty sand and then collapsed, exhausted, our bodies becoming covered with sand as we lay in the sun side by side. The surf touched our feet and left suds along our calves before retreating. The breeze felt cold against our naked bodies, still beaded with salt water yet drying fast.

She was becoming hysterical because we had come through our crisis and miraculously survived against the odds, and I was laughing so that my sides hurt.

High up on the beach two elderly ladies with their dogs were pointing at us and shrieking as if they had never seen two nude lovers lying on a beach, laughing together in the sunshine.

"Rachel, perhaps we should go up to the house and get dressed lest we be arrested for indecent exposure."

"I think it should be called 'decent exposure.'" She tried a faint smile at her own joke.

"You have uncommon sense for such a treacherous vixen as you turned out to be." I was being playful, but I still felt a bit of resentment. She shook her head and ruffled my hair.

She looked me in the eyes and said, "Race you!"

She was running for the beach house, her wet hair wrapped around her head and no hair whatsoever from her back and breasts to her toes. I followed sauntering at a leisurely pace, waving at the two ladies while they watched my member beating out the time. They were now covering their eyes, dogs barking at their sides non-stop. I laughed out loud at the dreams those two prurient ladies would have tonight and every night hereafter until as supercentenarians they finally realized what they had been missing all their lives. I thought of the Deputy Director of Operations watching Rachel and me from her lofty distance, going into conniptions and raging against the dynamics she herself had set in motion, jealous and envious and spiteful like the hag that she always had been.

I searched the house for Rachel, and I found her hiding and huddling in a ball in the large closet, weeping uncontrollably. I drew her up to my body and held her in my arms.

"I knew, love. I knew it all the time. Here, let me kiss your tears away. Oh, love. What would I ever do without you? Come now, come with me—let's take a shower."

We had a very long, warm, luxurious shower. We had never needed lessons in what to do to arouse each other. I had never needed pills or a special diet. She was the only recipe I needed, and she knew that.

We washed each other until we were fairly sure that no sand would abrade us when we proceeded to the next phase of our unspoken agenda. If she had ever been tense or afraid, there was no sign of that now. Her greatest secret, beyond all our intimate secrets that had been eliminated one by one, was now on the table for both of us to see. How much she had feared my discovery, I could not say. How much I repressed what I knew she was, I could not say. I can say that both of us were now free of illusions and deceptions. The most unlikely midwife to our love had, ironically, set us free. I did still hate that harridan Deputy Director of Operations with her red everything and her prying intelligence and her insatiable desire to pick and probe and needle. How could I blame her for sending her own protégé to me for tutelage? She knew I would not accept a protégé proffered by someone else. She knew that I had to make the discovery myself and learn to nurture and grow the protégé's talents without external pressures. She knew I would let down all my defenses and let the right person into my innermost soul. She knew more than I had ever given her credit for.

When I thought that Rachel had probably reported on my every move to my boss so that she knew exactly what I was doing at every stage of my operations and my personal life, I realized something else. No other form of teaching could compare to the instruction delivered to a person I genuinely loved. I had taught protégés before, but I never let them get as close as I had allowed Rachel to get. She became part of me, and then, gradually, she overtook me and finally she had become a free agent. How much of what we did together was us and how much was the result of the coaxing of the Wicked Witch of the East? Who could say for sure? Was Rachel's brilliance partly a result of the Deputy Director of Operations' percipient interjections? I might have become anxious about these matters, but strangely I did not.

Reviewing the bidding, I now had a fair idea of why Rachel was such a good all-around athlete, such a fine marksman, such an excellent analyst, such a fine strategic thinker, such a patient and thorough researcher, such an out of box operational player. She had laughed at bureaucracy. She had understood why I had to keep back information from my boss and why I had to turn all the credit for my operations to others. Had the Deputy Director of Operations coached Rachel to understand me before she ever met me? If so, just how much did my boss know about me herself? Would she have had to fantasize a relationship with me to get inside my soul as far as she apparently had done? I was genuinely impressed with the tyro and hag if so. If not, Rachel was good enough to discover how to play me all by herself. She had been as much on her own with me as she was with any of our targets. Was I no different to her really than her other targets?

"I know what you're thinking, Anderson." I felt her warm, small hand on my arm, gently tracing its outline from my elbow to my shoulder and my neck. She leaned over my head with her raven black hair falling over my face; she licked my ear and blew gently on it. Then she kissed my lips, and I smelled her panther's breath and looked into those blackest of eyes with their pupils dilated to the limit. She was looking right into my brain.

"There were times," I said, "that I thought you were a goddess sent to earth as a companion for me alone. No kidding." Rachel started tickling me as she always did when I became too serious.

"Stop tickling me while I explain something to myself. You don't even have to pay attention. If you don't stop that, I'll tickle you. There. Now stop laughing for a minute."

Rachel had backed off from her tickling assault and was now pretending to be the little angel with her hands neatly folded in her lap and her beautiful eyes fixed on mine.

"I had three theories about you. You were either the externalization of the perfect woman taken from my soul and like a succubus made flesh to torment me and devour me. Or you were the plant of some other agency meant to infiltrate my Agency to obtain all our secrets. Or you were what you seemed, a person who came into my life because you had no past but needed someone to take you to your future.

"Now I discover that you were all three, with the exception that you were a mole from my own Agency sent to keep tabs and to get instruction, probably in equal measure. No, I don't want you to explain yourself. Nothing about how you came to me or what your intent was or how it changes everything really matters to me now."

Rachel had begun to cry. Her shoulders were hunched forward, and she sobbed uncontrollably.

"Stop crying, please. Let me brush away your tears. Okay, I'll kiss them away."

"Please stop."

"No, I will not stop. You stop."

She shook her head sadly from side to side.

"No? Well, then. What I mean to say is that here we are after how many adventures and how many bouts of magnificent love making. Transporting? Nirvana-esque? Boring? How about pedestrian?"

That had the desired effect; Rachel had gritted her teeth and was now pounding my chest with her fists and kicking me.

"Stop pummeling me with your tiny fists and kicking me with those very tiny feet."

"They aren't very tiny." She became self-conscious and looked at her feet.

"Yes, they are tiny. See how they compare with mine? So! I have called you Rachel all these days. Will you tell me your real name, please? For me you will always be Rachel, as for you, I expect that I will always be whatchamacallit. Oh yes, Anderson. I am Anderson, always will be. And you are who? Andrea McGillicutty? Ubiquitous Gump?"

She laughed out loud appreciatively.

"Don't laugh, we can play this game all night."

She became serious again and tears streamed down her face.

"Now you're weeping again. I hate it when I make you cry. Please don't cry."

Rachel tried to stop sobbing, but the tears would not stop coming.

"All right, I will ask no more questions except for one. May I ask one more question? It's important to me."

She nodded.

"Yes? Will you, Rachel, marry me, Anderson, by any name at all?"

She nodded again in shocked delight.

"You are nodding yes. Is that a yes?"

She kept nodding, and her whole face was breaking into a radiant smile. Yet her tears now came in a torrent.

"I want the word, not a sobbing, nodding, shaking and trembling Keats-like kinesthetic answer, but a one word, definitive, absolute and forever answer."

I handed her a facial tissue. She took it and blew her nose. She shook her head as if to clear her mind. Her wet eyes sought mine to discover that I was totally serious about this question.

"Yes, I will marry you, you fool. I loved you before we ever met, and I will love you for all time. No one else will do. No one could ever do me like you do."

"So it is yes? Really it is?"

She picked up a pillow and started to hit me with it repeatedly.

"Stop hitting me with that pillow."

She smiled, got a determined look and started tickling me again.

"Now stop tickling me."

She redoubled her attack, now laughing with flashing eyes.

"I will call the harridan. I'll pick up my cell and call her and, well, I'll tell on you for a change. She has to know the truth, don't you think?"

She shook her head.

"No? She isn't your mother, is she? I don't think I could stand her as my mother-in-law."

She shook her head from side to side."

"No? Is your mother remotely like the harridan Harpy wicked witch tyro etcetera?"

Now she was smiling again. She shook her head.

"No? Well, I am glad about that. Not that it would matter."

Rachel was moving closer, and she threw her arms around me and kissed me. I had other things to say, so I put her at arm's length for a moment.

"Tell me, do you want the harridan to come to our wedding? And the Director too? How about the President?"

She was hitting me with her fists suddenly.

"No hitting! No?"

"No, silly!"

"Okay. Enough for now about our happily ever after thing?"

"Never. Never enough. Do I make you happy? Really?"

"You do make me happy."

She smiled seraphically and was getting ready to cry at the thought of our happiness. "Come here. And now let's return to basics. Like this."

I gently kissed each of her eyes.

"And this."

I now feasted greedily on her soft mouth.

"Mmmm."

Now she threw her arms around me and hugged me and kissed all over my face while I pulled her close to me.

"Yes and that," Rachel said as she melted into my arms.

"Nnnngh. Yes!"

Rachel Plays Backup

Rachel was one of the best Internet researchers I had ever known, not because she could find what you wanted, but because she could learn important things from open sources that no one knew were there in the first place. She searched laterally and ranged widely, connecting dots that she had only just imagined. Then she brought her data to life by finding meaningful connections. An example was Cabinda. How she found Cabinda beats me. She could not reconstruct her brain's complex process. When I understood what was packed into that one word, I was astonished. It ultimately led the Agency to a new appreciation for the West African offshore oil and gas industry.

Rachel was out running on the beach when I found her notes about Cabinda. I could not wait to talk with her about it. Upon her return, Rachel exuberantly exploded with information, and I had a hard time getting her to explain herself in a linear fashion. She was using the Vitamix to make herself a smoothie, and her hands were waving as she dropped the kiwi, the pineapple, and the Granny Smith apples into the whirling blender. When I did understand Rachel, I knew that she was onto something very big; the vulnerability of offshore oil and gas operations worldwide.

Rachel did not stop with Cabinda because she figured that Cabinda was a real place with an oil and gas signature that could fit many other real places too, like the Spratly Islands in the South China Sea, the Andaman Islands in the Indian Ocean, and off Cabo San Lucas in our own Gulf of California.

We had not planned to go fishing off Cabo, but on a hunch we took a week's vacation and drove down the length of Baja California to Cabo and rented a small cabana on the beach. By night, we made hot, passionate love. By day, we went fishing in a rented deep-sea fishing boat. We caught some fine Marlin, which we released alive into the warm blue water. We also got a lot of Mexican sunshine that made Rachel a bronze Greek statue only with tan lines and me a red lobster fringed with hair. We also scouted scattered oil exploration drilling rigs, and we marked them on our nautical charts with descriptive notations. They had no security whatsoever.

Rachel said that she saw a clear pattern in the vulnerabilities of offshore oil and gas operations. When we returned to the safe house in LA, Rachel asked many innocent questions that took us deep into research on drilling consortia, oil and gas partnerships, and the business of protecting offshore oil and gas infrastructure from the North Sea to Equatorial Guinea and Alaska to Indonesia. When she had done her calculations, Rachel said that she would like to go sailing in the Arabian Gulf. She was evidently entirely unfazed by her prior experience dealing with Arabs, but I wanted to be sure.

"Do you really want to deal closely with Arabs after what you've been through?"

"I won't judge an entire people based on one bad experience. Look, Anderson, we're both professionals. We take risks all the time. I won't just stop being an effective agent, and neither will you."

When I asked which Gulf Airlines flight we should book, she said, munching on her bagel with cream cheese, that we did not really need to go to the Gulf just yet. She wanted to do some more research first, and we might not need to go to the Gulf at all. I patiently waited while she continued to do her thinking and surfed myriad websites that gave her solutions. When she was ready, she laid everything out for me.

Rachel said that the world's biggest problem with offshore oil and gas was the largest company in the world, Saudi Aramco, whose ownership was largely held by the Kingdom of Saudi Arabia. If the Aramco oil and gas infrastructure could be attacked at five points simultaneously on land and sea, oil prices would skyrocket and within six months the global economy would crash. She had found a recipe for the Saudi version of September 11, 2001, right on the Internet. The scenario involved two hijacked aircraft striking both ends of the twin pipelines, which run East to West across northern Saudi Arabia. She had found the official report done in the aftermath of the most successful terrorist attack against Saudi Aramco in 2006. "No question," she said, "Aramco had been very lucky. With one additional vehicle fully laden with explosives, the terrorists would have accomplished their mission."

The bottom line, she continued, was to protect five thousand square miles of ocean area where the Saudi Aramco drilling and pumping operations took place. No maritime surveillance and interdiction capability of that scope had ever been attempted, not in the North Sea, the Caribbean Sea or anywhere else. Rachel said that the Aramco oil and gas infrastructure was a sitting duck. Saudi Arabia's greatest threat was Iran, and odds were that Iran was contemplating a coup of an attack. She saw a dozen scenarios that might work in the terrorists' favor. She convinced me of her argument, so I asked her to draft up her thoughts.

I figured that this line of thinking would have to be socialized among the analysts and strategized by the gray men of the CIA if we were to make any headway towards a solution. Building the infrastructure was not something our small group could handle on its own. I dreaded the prospect and had my doubts about the Agency's ability to go through with it.

Rachel thought that security, if it was provided by large private contractors, might cost five billion and take three years to execute. Then after it was in place, the security infrastructure would cost another $500 million each year for sustainment. Those numbers would not include expenses for support by the Royal Saudi Navy and Air Force and the Mukhabarat or Saudi Intelligence. She gave me a rueful look when she said that the 2006 terrorist attack had driven a wedge between Saudi Aramco and Saudi Intelligence that was widened by the recent, successful cyber attack against Saudi Aramco's computer networks. That rift was not good news.

As we talked through Rachel's analysis, I began to understand the geopolitical significance of Saudi oil and gas in a new light. World War III might be won and lost by introducing a few lines of malicious code in a computer network and by crashing two hijacked airliners into the east and west terminals of the most critical pipelines in the world. The Agency had a long history of providing security training and support for the Saudi Arabia, but the CIA alone could not provide the security required for the offshore operations. Rachel and I both worked around the clock to complete our report. Immediately after completing it, we sent the report to the boss under my name since Rachel technically did not exist.

We got the reaction I expected. On the phone, the harridan Deputy Director for Operations flew into one of her signature rages, complete with shrieking, yelling, cursing and bellowing. I could see the red dragon circling her desk and pounding on its surface. She first said that I must have been smoking too much weed. She then accused me of being way off the reservation. She finally asserted that hundreds of agents had already worked the problem of Aramco security from every conceivable angle. When I refused to stand down, I thought she was going to call down an air strike on the safe house. Instead, I heard a long silence on her end.

When she was done considering the implications, she said, "Anderson, your analysis is probably right, but I am going to have to get the right people on this. I will do that. For now, get back to doing what you were doing before you got this harebrained intuition. Stand down now! Do I make myself clear?"

I pressed 'END' and asked Rachel to pour us both some more iced tea.

Nothing the boss said or did could have been more incendiary for either of us than her simple order to 'stand down!' Rachel and I had one thing in common, and I liked us both for that: we never, ever stood down when national security was at stake. Some pundits might have argued that the Saudi oil and gas has nothing directly to do with U.S.

national security. Those halfwits are not thinking about what twenty-dollar-per-gallon gasoline would do to destroy the American economy, much less the economies of our allies in Europe, not to mention the strategic advantage that the Russian Federation would have after its major competitor was taken entirely offline. We did not exactly slouch in our chairs, stare listlessly out the window or fly into a black despondency. Instead, we brooded about the enormity of the threat and what we could do about it.

Suddenly Rachel became animated, jumping up, pacing the room and waving her arms. "Six years ago, ten of our best agents were killed in a terrorist attack on the Vinnell compound in Saudi Arabia. The terrorists who committed that attack have never been identified or apprehended. Someone ordered the attack and provided intelligence, materials, and logistical support. We should find and terminate the mastermind for all three of the terrorist attacks against Saudi Arabia. That might at least buy us time."

"Now," I said with a laugh, "all we have to do is locate the terrorist mastermind in the haystack, find a way to get close enough for a hit, and take him out."

Accordingly, we switched from looking at oil and gas vulnerabilities to looking for the wizard behind the magic curtain who would exploit those weaknesses to bring down the Saudi oil and gas capability and the world economy with it.

Sleep can provide the best thinking space to solve any significant problem. Rachel and I had used a special variant of the technique, which was adding lovemaking to the point of total exhaustion before falling asleep. We went to bed early, made love many times, and fell asleep in each other's arms sharing the sleep of the dead. At 4 a.m., I awakened and spoke the single word "Russia." I wrote it down so that I would not forget my insight and then fell fast asleep again.

Rachel nudged me at 7 a.m. when the external light began to flood our bedroom and threw one of her legs over mine. Her hand made my penis rise from its grave, and I turned to my goddess and began the day the way we both enjoyed. After our rousing exercise and shower, we ate yogurt and dates and drank coffee while I explained what I had learned in my sleep.

I said that we could learn a lot from negotiating with Iran about their nuclear capabilities. Iran would not come to any conclusions on its own. It depended on Russia particularly to block efforts to curtail its nuclear program. Historically Persia, which was present-day Iran without the Islamic overlay, fought by retreating, not advancing, and shooting arrows back at its pursuers. Iran was not the answer to our problem; Russia was. Our question was, who in Russia could trigger an Iranian attack on Saudi Arabia? I felt strongly that Iran would be capable of small, niggling attacks in specific locations. It would not be capable of making or even planning a grand play of the scope or dimensions of what we envisioned might happen.

"So you think that our mastermind for all three acts of terror might have come from a Russian who helped the terrorists attack Saudi Arabia?" She was genuinely interested.

"Of course, Rachel, I cannot be sure of that, but I am certain that September 11, 2001, was not an Iranian or Shiite operation. Rather, it was a Sunni and Saudi operation. It seems highly unlikely that the Sunnis and Saudis would attack Saudi Arabian oil and gas infrastructure. I think that the Saudi ballistic missiles and the weapons of the

American fleet in the Gulf will continue to keep Iran in check." Rachel seemed somewhat skeptical.

"So where are you heading with this line of reasoning?"

"For the grand play I submit that a Russian will orchestrate the plan and schedule; and that a terrorist organization will execute. The scary thing is that no one will have proof that Russia did anything to foment the attack that will give them the key to world domination through oil and gas."

"What else do you think, Anderson? How will we find the Russian who is the mastermind?" She was intrigued, but she needed to pin down what I said in a plan of action.

"That was my vision overnight, and it was confirmed in email traffic earlier this morning. If, as I suspect, a physical attack will be accompanied by a cyber attack on the networks that control all the Saudi Aramco pipelines, then the Russian cyber group that will initiate that attack will be the vanguard, and the leader of that cyber group is our target."

"Why should we focus only on the cyber attack?" Now Rachel was really skeptical. I had to be careful to make the dots connect for her as well as for myself.

"We'll focus on cyber for three reasons. First, the group can be located so that we can do our targeting. Second, if a cyber attack was properly executed, no physical attack on the infrastructure would be necessary; the cyber attack on the system control network would completely destroy the pipelines from the inside. Third, in order to execute a cyber attack on the infrastructure, an insider threat would have to be working in league with the Russian. I received an email this morning in response to our theories about an Aramco insider with a Russian contact. NSA has found the insider among the Saudi Aramco information technology personnel and traced him to the Russian. I think that we can take them out together."   I could tell that she liked the idea of focusing on the insider but still had doubts about execution.

"Since everything about cyber is carefully watched and monitored by people and software, how would you propose that we take out the insider?"

"That is where you come in, Rachel. If you are game, I'm going to plant you right where you can see who the insider is for yourself, at a bar in Amsterdam."   She said that she was game to do the job. I then told her how, according to the CIA's NSA liaison officer, an engineering group for Saudi Aramco's security had been dispatched to London. It was communicating with its home base in Riyadh on a unique encrypted circuit from London through Amsterdam to Saudi Arabia. That special circuit was being monitored both by British signals intelligence and by the NSA. From the decrypts gained from monitoring that and other circuits, my NSA liaison contact told me that an individual calling himself Samal Infada was sending portions of the information stream about Aramco's cyber vulnerabilities to his contact in Russia over the Joint Institute for Nuclear Research communications path, the Russian encrypted military railway circuit.

"Samal Infada is the insider. His correspondent is the Russian who will produce the malware and then orchestrate the cyber attack. This Russian is the notorious black hacker with the code name Boris K. The hacker is headed for Amsterdam now for a one-on-one meeting with Samal Infada, most likely to hand him a memory stick with malware on it for introduction into the Aramco system control network. Once again, Rachel, we will be entering the lion's den just in time to meet the lions. Our job will be to take out both Boris K and Samal Infada and to obtain the memory stick so that the NSA can analyze its contents and design neutralizing software."

"What is our intended approach?" Rachel asked.

"We know that Boris K is gay and promiscuous. We know that Samal Infada is heterosexual and promiscuous. We expect both men to be looking for sex partners in the love den of Amsterdam. For Boris K, we intend to serve Ryan Blomfeld. For Samal Infada, we shall serve Ryan's sister Ruth. If Samal Infada demurs, we shall serve you. You and Ruth Blomfeld will make the approach on Samal Infada together dressed to kill at the man's favorite watering hole, and the target will choose his fatal companion."

"Ryan and Ruth will depart for Amsterdam in one hour. Once in the Dutch city they'll occupy different rooms at the Terminus Hotel. They'll conduct initial surveillance of the Aramco building in the city and, if possible, they will begin tracking Samal Infada. When we arrive, we'll take Ryan's hotel room, and he will move in with his sister at the hotel. We four will design the schedule and the means of execution. When we have completed our mission, we plan to exfiltrate by the fastest available means. All modes of transport are being considered. In the worst case, we will depart by different means to avoid the opposition. We expect that the two targets will be carefully watched by Russian intelligence since this cyber operation is under the control of them. Here is a picture of Samal Infada. We don't know what Boris K looks like."

I handed Rachel the insider's picture. She examined it carefully. After we had both memorized the insider's picture, we burned it.

I made our flight arrangements, and we flew to Amsterdam by the fastest available connecting flights. Ruth and Ryan had arrived in Amsterdam as we had planned, and they were now lodging at the Terminus Hotel. Ruth had followed Samal Infada from the Aramco building to his favorite watering hole. He was drinking alone at the bar when she left it. Ruth said that Ryan was positioned to be ready to move right in on the Russian at the first indication that Boris K made contact with Samal Infada.

When we asked Ruth what means of assassination she had chosen, she held out two syringes and, with a grim smile, said, "Welcome to Amsterdam, the heroin overdose capital of Europe."

We dropped our luggage in Ryan's room, and then we proceeded to the bar to catch the action as it unfolded.

Boris K approached Samal Infada at 10 p.m. at the bar. There was no mistaking the Russian's nationality since he had a Slavic geek signature with hair slicked back over his head and a necklace with an icon of St. Cyril. Boris K slipped Samal Infada the thumb drive clumsily. Ryan moved in on Boris K like the perfect gay lounge lizard eyeing its prey. Ruth and Rachel moved into position on both sides of Samal Infada. The two men, who had just consummated the reason for their meeting, could not believe their luck. Unfortunately for them, they decided to indulge in a little sex to celebrate. I did not perceive any surveillance in place, so I signaled the 'all clear' by opening a newspaper and holding it in front of my face. Boris K went with Ryan to the Terminus Hotel, where he booked a room for the evening. After some deliberation, Samal Infada chose Ruth Blomfeld, not Rachel, as his evening's pleasure companion, and he walked her to the same Terminus Hotel where they entered her room.

Rachel and I went to Ryan's room to wait for the outcome. We did not have long to wait. Ryan appeared looking disheveled to announce that Boris K was out cold with an overdose of heroin coursing through his veins. The man would be dead in half an hour. He then said he would check on his sister. He boldly banged on the door of his sister's room and acted as if he were his sister's pimp. He bellowed that he wanted her to open the door and show him the money.

When Samal came to open the door, his face met Ryan's iron fist. He fell onto the floor in a heap. Ruth retrieved the precious memory stick from the insider's pocket and put it into her handbag. Brother and sister then lifted the unconscious man and took him, with one arm over each of their shoulders as if he were drunk, to the room where Boris K lay. They put the insider on the bed beside his contact.

Without any hesitation, they gave him an overdose of heroin that they had prepared for him. Satisfied with their work and having assured themselves that the men had died, they photographed the touching scene with Ryan's cell phone camera. They closed the locked door as they left, leaving the key inside with the two corpses. The siblings walked to Ryan's room where Rachel and I were waiting for them. With a wink, Ruth gave me the thumb drive that she had removed from Samal Infada's pants pocket.

We guessed that the corpses would not be discovered until late the next morning. The cause of death for each would not be perceived as assassination but as an assignation during which two unfortunate heroin overdoses occurred. Ruth then returned to her room, picked up her things and checked out of the hotel in a leisurely fashion at the same time her brother did. The siblings made their way to Amsterdam Airport Schiphol where they booked the earliest available flights to the U.S. via London. Meanwhile Rachel and I, who had not checked into the Terminus Hotel, carried our luggage outside the hotel and took a cab to the rail station where we booked first-class passage with sleeper accommodations to Paris on the overnight train. We were not followed all the way to the Charles de Gaulle Airport, where we were ticketed business class to the USA.

It bothered me that we had not encountered Russian intelligence surveillance for the meeting at the bar in Amsterdam. Could the meeting have been unsanctioned by Russian intelligence? Could the entire cyber plan of the grand operation to bring down the pipelines and destroy the global economy have been a purely commercial venture between two greedy little persons? We would probably never know the answers to those questions. We also would not know anything about the contents of the thumb drive that had been passed by Boris K to the insider. That was because I handed the precious cargo to the NSA liaison officer in the baggage claim area at JFK when we had arrived there. I recognized him because the officer stood like a cigar-store Indian, holding in two hands a sign that read "Ride?" in black letters on a white background. For some reason, Rachel found this to be hysterical. I was amused too, but I affected not to be concerned to find my companion doubled over in laughter in a public place. When she regained her composure, I took her arm with a straight face, and we proceeded to the departure ticket counter to book our flight back to LAX. Ten hours later we found ourselves back in our safe house where we had started.

We were exhausted on our arrival. While we enjoyed glasses of cold Chablis, for some reason I thought of the farce of the shoe bomber. How many espionage tales were as ridiculous as that incident, rather than tragic? I wished that many more would be as farcical as that one. Rachel rubbed her naked foot up my leg, and we were suddenly shifting to a new key. I decided to play our recording of Puccini's Tosca with Tito Gobbi as Scarpia and Maria Callas as Tosca. It sounded simply divine on our Bose speakers. Transported, I listened straight through from overture to the final, devastating curtain. The work was magnificent, as always. Rachel had fallen asleep mid-way through, so in the silence that followed the opera, I gently lifted her in my arms and took her to our bed, fluffed her pillow, tucked her in and kissed her good night gently on her forehead.

I went to my computer and found multiple emails, one from Ruth updating me on their safe arrival back home. The second was from my NSA liaison officer saying thanks for the package. It had been received as planned and was subsequently hand-delivered to the NSA analysis group. The last was, unsurprisingly, from the harridan Deputy Director of Operations ranting that I had not properly signed my timecard—again. I replied to the Blomfelds that Rachel and I were safe. I sent a brief thank you note to the NSA liaison officer. I responded to the Deputy Director for Operations that I could not encrypt her non-existent enclosure. I then sent a perfunctory email to my Agency support Team that I was back in battery and ready for action.

Rachel Ties the Knot

The Agency feels and operates a lot like a large, secular religious order, and the priests and nuns of this polyglot, global order comprise the best and brightest of their generations, an enduring, secretive group set apart from the rest by design. Some families look back upon three generations of CIA officers; other families have twenty or thirty siblings, cousins, aunts, uncles, nephews, nieces, grandfathers, grandmothers and so forth in the clandestine service fulfilling a broad range of functions from top management to janitorial and secretarial positions. Many agents have Agency spouses though discussions at their dinner tables are not supposed to have any hint of shop talk, which is verboten. I was once acquainted with a man and wife who knew that their spouse was employed by the Agency, but each had no idea what the other did within the Agency.

I had asked Rachel to marry me, and she had said yes. We each knew that our beloved worked for the Agency, and we worked together daily and most intimately with the cognizance and explicit sanction of our harridan boss. That sticklike creature all dressed in crimson like a Cardinal of the Church had infiltrated my Agent lover Rachel into my life and private operations. She did it for two antithetical reasons. First, she wanted me to become the mentor for her female protégé and teach the young lady all my hard-earned tricks. I gave the woman everything I had and helped make her an excellent agent, not knowing that she was already a CIA counterintelligence officer. Second, without my knowledge or consent, the harridan used Rachel to keep tabs on me as if I were some distrusted foreign agent or rogue, criminal operative and not a patriotic officer doing his best to serve our national security community. I felt unappreciated and a little bitter at the distrust my boss had shown.

Rachel became my girl Friday, right hand, helpmeet, partner, friend and, yes, my lover. This while she watched and spied on me, reported everything I said and did, photographed me in all kinds of incriminating and embarrassing poses, and tempted me with her sensuous, devilish ways. I was so angry when my deep suspicions had been verified by the harridan Deputy Director of Operations' own admission that I tried to swim to China in atonement for my sins against myself and all that I stood for. Only having my angel swim out to lure me back to sanity saved me from certain suicide. It was then that I knew that I could not do without her. I needed Rachel desperately, and I asked her to be mine forever. I asked her this knowing that she was a deceptive, lying, treacherous, no good, stinking liar and, of all things, a spy. But then it does take one to know one in this business. I suppose I deserved what I got, and I know that I got much more than I deserved.

Our wedding service was a simple civil ceremony at the Los Angles Court House. Four witnesses to our nuptials signed the document that proclaimed our status so that we could get the advantages of Agency spousal benefits and all the rest. Ruth and Ryan Blomfeld, Rosa Sanchez and the Wicked Witch of the East all signed as witnesses. Three smiled, one cackled. After all the oaths and signatures, I kissed the blushing bride. We invited our guests to a small reception at the rear of a hamburger joint in downtown LA. There we six ate burgers and fries and Cokes. Afterward, Rachel and I were surprised to find that my Jag had been decorated with shaving cream and crepe paper. The scrawl read, "Just Married" and "Ride?"

Rice was thrown, cheers ensued, and we drove off into the tyrannous Southern California sunshine. Our elite honeymoon suite, aka the safe house at the beach, was ready for us just as it always had been with our computers blinking and our large screen displays showing the international and financial news in real time. The only exceptions were a large basket of flowers on our kitchen table with a note from the Blomfelds, a bottle of champagne in the refrigerator with a note from Rosa Sanchez and the returned timecard on my pillow with the yellow sticky note that read, "Sign Here" with a jagged arrow. The sticky note was signed "DDO" with a winking frowny face, the semicolon followed by the open paren.

Rachel laughed so hard that she cried. I did the reverse, and that confirmed how we complemented each other. If she were standing on a street corner tomorrow and I saw her knowing all that I know now, I would still answer her "Ride?" sign with the same gallant gesture that meant, "Climb right in and let's ride!"

Glossary of Acronyms

Agency - CIA

BZ - Bravo Zulu [Allied Tactical Publication - 1 code for "well done"]

CIA - Central Intelligence Agency

CNN - Cable News Network

CU2 N30 - Chat term for "See you two in thirty minutes"

DDO - Deputy Director of Operations [of CIA]

DNA - Deoxyribonucleic Acid

DVM - Doctor of Veterinary Medicine

EU – European Union

IMOK - Chat term meaning "I am okay."

IP - Internet Protocol

IT - Information Technology

KKK - Chat term meaning "three persons are okay"

KGB - Komitet Gosudarstvenoy Besopasnosti [Russian for "Committee for State Security"]

LAX - Los Angeles International Airport

L - Chat term meaning "Love"

LGBT - Lesbian Gay Bisexual Transvestite

LMAO - Chat term meaning "Laughing my ass off"

NSA - National Security Agency

PRC - People's Republic of China

R&R - Rest and Relaxation

Red Queen - The deranged character in Alice in Wonderland

TKS - Chat term meaning "Thanks"

USSR - Union of Soviet Socialist Republics

VEE - Venezuelan Equine Encephalitis

XTC - Chat term meaning "Ecstasy"

XX - Chat term meaning "Kiss, kiss"

XXX - Chat term meaning "Kiss, kiss, kiss"

About the Author

E.W. Farnsworth

E.W. Farnsworth is a former military officer, contractor, and a current consultant to law enforcement and intelligence agencies. He lives and writes in sunny Arizona.

Farnsworth's collection of crime stories, *John Fulghum Mysteries,* will appear from Zimbell House Publishing LLC in December 2015. His collected westerns and spy stories will be separately published under contract later this year.

Bitcoin Fandango, Farnsworth's picaresque novel about global intrigue in cryptocurrency enforcement appeared from Greenman Arizona Press in March 2015, and is now on sale worldwide.

Farnsworth has had fifty short stories published in numerous anthologies in the U.K. and the U.S. during 2015; including many in Zimbell House Publishing, LLC anthologies. Some of E.W. Farnsworth's sci-fi stories and modern fables are available online from Ether Books, and Jotters United in the U.K. and Fictuary.com in the U.S. Two of his John Fulghum mysteries will be available online in 2015 at IndelibleCHAOS in India.

E.W. Farnsworth is now working on an epic poem, *The Voyage of the Spaceship Arcturus*, about the future of humankind when humans, avatars, and artificial intelligence must work together to instantiate a second Eden after the Chaos Wars bring an end to life on Earth.

An interview with E.W. Farnsworth is featured on the Zimbell House Publishing, LLC website, http://www.zimbellhousepublishing.com/author-spotlight/e-w-farnsworth//

For continuous updates on the current and forthcoming works of E.W. Farnsworth, please see his website: www.ewfarnsworth.com.

Reading Group Guide

Discussion Questions

1. When Rachel was first introduced, were you suspicious of her identity? If so, did you suspect her to be an enemy spy?

2. How did you react when Rachel went off on her own, without telling Anderson? Did you find her actions brave, rash, headstrong, shortsighted, or praiseworthy?

3. How did the relationship between Anderson and Rachel change throughout the book?

4. Ruth repeatedly killed her targets without hesitation. Did you agree or disagree with her harsh behavior? Were her actions warranted?

5. What was your favorite scene in the book, and why did you choose this scene?

6. Did you enjoy the romance or thriller aspects of the book more?

7. Sex plays a prominent role in both the story and the characters' relationships. How did you feel about the use of sex? Did you find it effective, or did it detract from the novel?

8. Did you find the characters and their actions believable? Were there times you were surprised by the characters' actions or thought they should have behaved in a different way?

9. When Rachel's true identity was revealed, did your view of her change? Did you think more or less of her?

10. How would the story differ if it was told from Rachel's point of view instead?

A Note from the Publisher

Dear Reader,

Thank you for reading E.W. Farnsworth's novel, *Engaging Rachel.* We feel the best way to show appreciation for an author is by leaving a review. You may do so on Goodreads, Amazon.com, Kindle.com, or Smashwords.com.